Waltham For...

Please return this item by the last... renewed unless require...

D0352643

Feb 2021		

Need to renew your books?
http://www.walthamforest.gov.uk/libraries or
Dial 0333 370 4700 for Callpoint – our 24/7 automated telephone renewal line. You will need your library card number and your PIN. If you do not know your PIN, contact your local library.

For Harriet and all the other brilliantly
wonderful children out there who love books.

NEW FRONTIER PUBLISHING

First published in Great Britain in 2020
by New Frontier Publishing Europe Ltd.,
Uncommon, 126 New King's Road, London SW6 4LZ

www.newfrontierpublishing.co.uk

ISBN: 978-1-912858-49-1

Illustrated by Beatriz Castro
Text copyright © Helen Castles, 2020
Illustrations copyright © New Frontier Publishing, 2020

Edited by Stephanie Stahl
Designed by Rachel Lawston

SCOOP McLAREN
· WAVES OF MYSTERY ·

Helen Castles

CHAPTER ONE

PRINCE OF THE WAVES SAILS INTO SURFING SEMI–FINAL

By Scoop McLaren

Higgity Harbour is abuzz with news that thirteen-year-old surfing sensation, Fletcher Stein, nicknamed 'In Flight', has won the last heat of the Monster Wave Supreme Grommet Title. The competition was held yesterday right here at Five-Mile Beach, where he cemented his place in the upcoming semi-final!

Stein, who has been taming waves since he was just five years old, left competitors in his wake, barely making an error throughout the whole competition.

Stein blitzed each of his twenty-minute stints to line up against Haywire Bay's best junior boy surfer, Andy Sadler, 'The Shark'. Sadler put in a near faultless performance, but it wasn't good enough to take the heat away from a title-hungry Stein.

'I've never seen a more talented junior surfer,' Stein's coach, Ted McLaren. said. 'If he remains focused and determined, we could be watching young Fletcher on the surfing world stage in the not-too-distant future.'

When asked what Stein's secret weapon is, McLaren was tight-lipped.

'I can't divulge that sort of information,' he said, 'but I will say he has a particular penchant for avocado and chocolate sauce sandwiches!'

For Stein, the allure of the waves is easily explained.

'I'm at home in the ocean, there's no better feeling than riding a massive wave,' he told *Click!*.

With a record £3,000 in prize money up for grabs, the ultimate winner will walk away with more than just a shiny silver trophy.

Click! will be at the forefront of all the action with online updates and more exclusive interviews, covering the competition until the winner is crowned.

Editor's note: *Click!* does not endorse the eating of avocado and chocolate sauce sandwiches and, in fact, finds the suggestion of any such concoction to be totally and utterly gross!

My online newspaper *Click!* has gone national!

My reputation as a dedicated, problem-solving detective editor is earning me fans from far and wide! My roving reporter on the ground, Evie Andrews, and I get *loads* of messages from people on a daily basis, encouraging us in our pursuit for the truth. ☺ Totally amazing!

After we exposed the mischievous Sonny Fink, evil editor of *The Dark Times*, *Click!*'s popularity skyrocketed, and we now have a solid base of regular readers from all over the country.

We hit an exciting milestone just yesterday when the paper was viewed an incredible 6,123 times! That may sound a little scary, to have *that* many people reading over your every word, but Evie and I agree that the more readers we can reach with our stories, the better. Working on *Click!* every day is so much fun!

Summer holidays are almost at an end (yuck!). This year Dad wanted to teach me and Evie how to surf. He's an awesome surfer – he won a few titles of his own as a teenager – and he's a pretty good instructor too. Even though I'm nowhere near as good as my friend Fletcher, it's still super cool fun being out amongst the waves.

Fletcher has been staying with Dad and I here in sunny Higgity Harbour. His mum (Dad's childhood best friend, Felicity) and his dad, Clive, are research scientists, currently on a tour of Antarctica.

Fletcher and Dad love to hit the surf. This summer my dad's been busy training him, and Fletcher has become the red-hot favourite to win the surfing title.

♥

Evie and I strolled along the sand with the remains of the afternoon sun dancing on our cheeks. We were on our way to the surf shop café to meet up with Fletcher who was there to talk semi-final tactics with ex-surfing pro, Mr Mack.

'Three *thousand* pounds in prize money,' Evie said, her eyes whirling with excitement as she skipped along the sand. 'Can you even imagine? What would you do with all that money, Scoop?'

The shoreline was almost deserted apart from some lingering beach bums savouring the last of a perfect summer's day.

'Hmm…' I tried to come up with some

extraordinarily amazing way to spend the money, but in the end, I simply sighed and said, 'I think I'd just give it to my dad to keep for me until I get older.'

'*Bo-ring*,' Evie sang.

'That's *after* I take a trip to Spain to visit my mum. First class, of course.'

'Of course,' Evie laughed. 'You miss your mum, don't you, Scoop?'

I smiled. 'Always.'

Mum is still living in Spain where she works as a dog trainer. She trains dogs to appear in movies. Mum once trained a dog to do a back flip off a moving train onto the back of a truck! Sometimes I walk Mrs Lumgarten's Labrador, Daisy, and I can't even get her to roll over.

Mum messages me every single day and we video chat at least three times a week, but I still miss her so much. She's really funny and kind and smart. All these things Dad says I get from her. Maybe someday my mum will come back to Higgity Harbour to live, but since she and Dad don't get along any more, I'm not holding my breath.

We were still making plans for the three thousand pounds that we were certain *not* to win when we arrived at the surf shop café. Evie was jumping around and giggling about how she would probably blow the whole lot on a lifetime supply of chocolate malt milkshakes when she ran smack, bang into a tall, thin, gangly man, dressed sharply in a navy suit and a dark red tie with pictures of little yachts all over it. He was hurriedly leaving the surf shop café.

'Oh,' Evie cried as she bounced back and stared up into the stranger's little black eyes. 'I'm… I'm sorry, I didn't—'

'Watch where you're going, young miss,' the man said in an irritated tone.

I looked down at his shiny black shoes that I guessed were not at all sand proof and I wondered why such an official-looking gentleman would be at a hangout like Mr Mack's café.

The man brushed us both aside like we were annoying little flies. He then turned and glared at Mr Mack. 'This isn't the last you'll be seeing of me,' he said firmly.

Evie and I gazed over at each other. *Yikes!*

We watched the stranger leave. He kept dusting the sand off his shoes and muttering under his breath until he reached his sparkly black sports car that was parked nearby.

'Who was *that*?' Evie asked.

'Beats me,' I shrugged.

Sitting on one of the surf shop benches, we found Mr Mack staring aimlessly out of the window with a far-off look in his eyes. When he spied us, he livened himself up and went to work on wiping down the counter.

'Where's Fletcher?' he grumbled.

Evie mocked quietly. '*Oh, hello, girls, lovely to see you. How are you both today? Fine thanks, Mr Mack. How's your good self?*' I stifled a giggle.

'I guess Fletcher's late,' I told him, taking a seat on a stool at the counter.

'Well I don't have all day,' Mr Mack grumbled. 'If he wants me to help him win this tournament, he needs to learn to be on time,' he spat, shaking his head. 'That boy's never on time lately.'

He turned his back on us and madly straightened the souvenirs that were caked with dust on a shelf behind the counter.

'Who was that man?' Evie asked him, jumping onto the seat next to me. 'The guy with the shiny shoes and the fancy car and the frightfully bad attitude? I've never seen him around here before. Is he a friend of yours, Mr Mack?'

I shot her a look. 'Evie, it's not polite to stick your nose into other people's business,' I whispered.

'But we're *always* sticking our noses into other people's business,' she protested, twirling around and around on her seat. 'It's what we do.'

'*No*, what we do is investigate stories. In the interests of the public.'

'Huh, is that what you call it?' Mr Mack said before turning around and leaning over the counter at us. 'Little girls like you two should be seen and not heard.' Then he turned his attention directly towards Evie whose seat twirling had come to an abrupt halt. 'Especially *you*.'

Evie folded her arms and huffed. Then she took her backpack off and sat it on the counter.

'Can I interest you in some chocolate bars?' she asked Mr Mack, pulling a box of the sugary treats out. 'We're raising money for our Girl Scout troop. How many will you buy? One? Two?'

'None,' Mr Mack gruffly said, and Evie's face fell.

'But it's for a good cause,' she continued.

'I don't like chocolate. Can't stand the taste of it,' he replied.

Her eyes widened. 'You *don't* like chocolate? Mr Mack, is there *anything* you enjoy in life?' she asked.

'Yes – peace and quiet!' he shot back. Then he turned on his heel and disappeared into the kitchen.

Evie turned to me. '*Doesn't* like chocolate?'

I shrugged.

'No wonder he's so grumpy all the time,' she said.

♥

It was fifty-five minutes later when Fletcher sailed into the surf shop café, chewing on gum and looking none too bothered about being so dreadfully late. Lucky for him he was a surfer and not a reporter – he'd never make a deadline!

'Hiya, guys,' he said, plonking himself down into a booth. 'What's up?'

'What's up? You're fifty-five minutes late, Fletcher, that's what's up,' I told him. 'Where have you been? Mr Mack is *not* in a good mood. He said to tell you that he's out the back, emptying the garbage, and that you had better have a very good excuse as to why you weren't here an hour ago or you can forget all about him helping you train for the tournament.'

Fletcher frowned. 'No, I'm not late.' He took his phone from his pocket and checked the time. 'I'm actually five minutes early.'

'You were supposed to meet us here at four o'clock, Fletch,' Evie said, pointing to a clock in the shape of a surfboard on the wall. 'It's almost five!'

'Oh no, not again,' he whined. 'This is the second time this week that this has happened. I almost missed my heat because of this stupid phone!'

'Can I see it?' I asked, bouncing off my stool and sliding into the booth opposite him.

It looked brand new, shiny, and the screen was in tiptop shape with not a scratch on it. Just the wrong time.

'My dad just bought it for me so that we can keep in touch while he and my mum are overseas,' Fletcher said.

'Tell me how you almost missed the heat?' I asked.

'Well, yesterday morning, I went for my usual surf. I left my phone and my wallet in my shoes on the beach like I always do and then—'

'When you came back, the time on your phone was running an hour late?'

'Right. Except I didn't work that out until later. I thought I had a good hour up my sleeve and was demolishing a hot dog here at the café when Mr Mack told me that I'd better get a hurry on.'

'Otherwise you would have missed out on the heat entirely?'

'Probably, yeah. Then I fixed the time on the phone

and… now it's happened again,' he said. 'Stupid, dud phone.'

'I don't think so,' I said, handing the phone back. 'I mean, I don't think your phone is the problem. I've got a funny feeling and my funny feelings are rarely wrong.'

'Huh?'

'She's right,' Evie nodded, jumping up from the counter. 'Her funny feelings are usually spot on. In fact, I've never known anyone to have better funny feelings than Scoop!'

Fletcher looked confused. 'A funny feeling about what?' he asked.

'What if someone is trying to stop you from competing in the surfing competition, Fletch?' I said. Fletcher looked even more confused. Suddenly Mr Mack came back in and told us that he had to close the café early and that he would not be able to help Fletcher today. So the three of us decided to make our way back home.

♥

We walked along The Esplanade. It was getting dark. The sun had gone for the day and the air was still and calm. Night was drawing in and as we passed along, the street lamps began to illuminate, one by one.

I was totally serious about the whole situation, but Fletcher just laughed. 'Let me see if I understand this. Someone's out to get me? That's what you're saying?' he asked.

I nodded. 'That's one theory, yes.'

'That is absolutely daft, Scoop, even for someone like you,' he said.

'What do you mean *someone like me*?' I asked, folding my arms and kicking stones along the way.

How rude! We've known each other since we were babies, he even calls my dad 'Uncle Ted', and here he was, questioning me and my sixth sense. The very same sixth sense that has helped me solve trillions of mysteries in the past. Well, maybe not trillions, but an awful lot!

He could see I was getting annoyed, so toned his amusement down a little.

'Look,' he started out, his face softening, 'I understand that you have a suspicious mind and that you probably have to because of your newspaper gig and solving mysteries and catching criminals, which, by the way, I think is totally cool and all…'

'Thank you.'

'But a dodgy phone is the only problem I have at the moment,' he smiled. 'Nobody is… out to get me. In fact, apart from this useless phone, it's pretty much been a perfect summer.'

'Okay. If you say so,' I shrugged. I pulled back and let Fletcher and Evie continue on ahead of me.

Maybe Fletcher was right? Maybe this time I was wrong? Perhaps me and my sixth sense *should* just be on holiday and not be so suspicious all the time?

I listened as Fletcher told Evie about Kenny Dixon snaking some guy out in the surf this morning.

'Surfing terms – it's like a whole other different language!' Evie beamed. I could tell she was impressed. 'So, what exactly is *snaking*?'

'Well, snaking is when another surfer drops in and steals your wave,' Fletcher told her. He was jumping around in front of her, his face alive with talk of the thing he's most passionate about. What I looked like, I supposed, when I'm telling someone about *Click!*.

In the distance I could hear the faint whirring of a motorcycle travelling up the road behind us.

'And other surfers, they don't like this? When you snake them?' Evie asked.

'Are you kidding?' Fletcher cried, grabbing his

head dramatically with both hands. 'They hate it! It's the absolute worst thing you can do to another surfer.'

'Wow, surfing is *so cool*. Scoop's dad is teaching both of us and I absolutely love it!' she said. Then she held her arms out, like she was about to take flight, mimicking herself atop her surfboard. 'Sometimes it feels like I'm flying out there,' she beamed.

'I know, right?' Fletcher replied.

Fletcher and Evie's chatter was drowning in the sound of the motorcycle, roaring and drawing ever closer. I turned to see the headlight, veering up the road towards us.

'Kenny better hope he doesn't run into that guy again,' Evie said, 'or—'

But that's all I heard.

Before I knew it, the motorcycle was upon us. I watched as it veered off the road with one swift movement and onto the footpath.

It's headed straight for us!

I turned to see a look of horror etched on Evie and Fletcher's faces. They were glued to the spot, as was I, barely comprehending the scene unfolding before us.

Then something inside jolted me into action.

'Look out!' I shouted as I jumped out of the way. It all happened in a flash. Fletcher grabbed Evie and flung her out of the motorcycle's path before he too jumped to safety. The bike sped past us in a blur, but so close I could've reached out and touched it.

The three of us landed on the grass, the contents of my backpack strewn all over the lawn.

Without even thinking about it, I immediately went into reporter mode. Still on the ground, I reached over and grabbed for my phone. I quickly lined the bike up and took pictures of it as it sped off into the darkness.

Click, click, click!

'Did you get the licence plate, Scoop?' Evie asked as Fletcher helped her to her feet.

'No,' I replied. 'It was covered. Darn! Everyone okay?'

Evie and Fletcher looked at each other, still stunned by what had just happened.

'Yes, I'm okay,' Evie replied, patting herself down.

'Me... me too,' Fletcher gulped.

I got to my feet and walked over to him. His sandy blond hair was all ruffled and he had dirt plastered down the side of his arm. Considering that we all took some pretty heavy tumbles, we were lucky as there wasn't a visible scratch among us.

Fletcher turned towards me, his face flushed and

his voice shaking. 'What... what just happened? Who *was* that?'

'I don't know. This is very strange! Maybe someone really does *not* want you in that semi-final, Fletcher,' I said, brushing dust from my T-shirt. 'And if that's the case, it looks as if they'll stop at nothing to make that happen!'

CHAPTER TWO

'I'm afraid the picture's too blurry, kids. Nice try though, Scoop,' Sergeant Andrews said when Dad took us to the police station. 'Is there anything you guys can remember about the bike? Any specific or unusual details?'

We were sitting in Sergeant Mick Andrews' office, a place I'd been to a million times before with Evie. We'd been fingerprinted and had our mugshots taken – all in fun, of course – but never had I been there as a witness to a possible crime. I was used to investigating mysteries, not being a part of them!

'It all happened so fast,' Fletcher said, with Evie nodding in agreement.

'It was so scary, Dad. He came up behind us, quick as lightning,' Evie cried. 'Then like a shot, he was gone.'

'Or *she*,' I added.

'Right,' Sergeant Andrews said. He leaned over his desk and did the dad thing by giving Evie's hand a squeeze. Then he cleared his throat and got back to business. 'What about you, Scoop? Any details at all about the bike?'

I thought back. 'Maybe… it had some sort of bird on it. Like a… hawk or… an eagle. On a badge, on the side. Maybe…'

'That's good. That's something to keep an eye out for,' he said.

'Do you really think this rider was aiming for the kids though, Mick?' Dad asked.

'I think a mechanical failure is more likely, Ted, or simply a lapse in concentration. Then the rider probably got scared by the near miss and took off. I'll need to get whoever it was off the streets though. We can't have this sort of negligence.'

'Scoop has a theory,' Evie piped up.

'Really? Well, what is it, Scoop?' Sergeant Andrews asked.

'She thinks the rider was aiming for Fletcher.'

'You do?' Dad asked me. 'But why?'

'She thinks—'

'Okay, Evie,' Sergeant Andrews said. 'Scoop can speak for herself.'

Evie looked at me and smiled. 'Sorry.'

'That's okay,' I said. 'Well, Fletcher has a great chance to win not only the upcoming semi-final, but the whole competition. And while it might just be a kids' surfing competition and a bit of fun to most, lots of these families take this opportunity very seriously. So, I think… whoever was on that motorcycle knew *exactly* what they were doing. I think they were aiming to either take Fletcher out of the competition, or, at the very least, scare him into thinking he's now a target, hoping he'll feel unsettled or even withdraw his entry.'

Dad frowned. 'I just can't believe that anyone in Higgity Harbour would do such a thing,' he said.

'It might not be a Higgity Harbour resident, Dad,' I told him. 'There are lots of out-of-towners here, many of whom came here specifically for their kids to compete in the surfing comp.'

'I… I guess it's a possibility,' Dad said. 'What do you think about all this, Fletch?'

Fletcher squirmed in his seat and then sighed. 'Well, some parents really *do* take this stuff seriously. I mean, I've won close to twenty thousand pounds over the past two years, just surfing in comps. Mum and Dad have the money put away, in a special bank account for when I'm older.'

Evie's eyes widened, and she sat forward in her chair. 'You *have*?' she asked. 'Jeepers creepers, Fletcher – you're rich!'

'Evie,' her dad said, motioning for her to pipe down.

'I didn't believe Scoop at first either,' Fletcher continued. 'I mean, nothing like this has ever happened to me before, but…' he shrugged.

Dad looked at Sergeant Andrews. 'What do you make of all this, Mick?' he asked. 'Do you really think there's anything to worry about?'

'Well, I think the best thing to do from now until this whole competition is over is to err on the side of caution,' Sergeant Andrews said.

'Huh?' Evie frowned.

'Just be careful, dear daughter,' he said before turning his attention to Fletcher and I. 'You two as well. No… sneaking around investigating, okay, Scoop?' I started rolling my eyes but then my dad gave me a look – the look he always gives me to let me know he's not at all impressed with my behaviour but is too polite to say so in public. 'Leave the investigating to me this time,' Sergeant Andrews continued. 'You three just stick together, let us know where you are at *all* times, keep an eye out for each other, call me if anything peculiar happens, and enjoy what's left of the summer holidays.'

♥

I've never been taken off an investigation before.

I can understand Sergeant Andrews' reasoning – he just wants to keep us safe – but if someone is out to get to my friend, I can hardly just sit back and do nothing. I'm Scoop McLaren, Detective Editor! ☺

I was in my bedroom, sprawled out on the floor with my laptop in front of me, messing about with tomorrow's front page, when my phone chimed. It was a message from Evie.

Well, we can't just sit back and do nothing, no matter what my dad says.

Amazing! I wrote back. **I was just thinking the same thing.** ☺

Cool! What now, boss?

I had a think. **It's time we got to know Fletcher's competition a little better.**

Right! Speaking of, where's Fletch?

He and Dad are downstairs watching a movie. A comedy by the sounds of it.

Are you going to let him in on the plan?

Hmm… I don't think so. Probably better that he's not distracted by all of this. Let him concentrate on the surf comp.

Good idea!

Meet me at the beach in the morning? 7 a.m.? The surfers usually get together after a surf. We'll mingle, see what we can find out.

Sounds good!

See you then! YFIS, DE.

Evie and I always sign our messages off with DE for detective editor, RR for roving reporter and YFIS – it means Your Friend In Sleuthing!

See you at 7 a.m. sharp! YFIS, RR.

♥

As the sun was rising, the surfers crawled out of the ocean like a legion of ants in their black wetsuits.

Evie and I sat on the shore, armed with our voice recorders and notebooks, ready to do some digging.

'There they are, Evie,' I said, pointing to a gangly-looking boy with stringy brown hair and a shorter kid with a jet black mop. 'The tall one's Tom Broadmeyer and the other is Wallace Arnold. They are Fletcher's main competition.'

'Right,' she said, jumping up and brushing sand from her skirt.

'I'll take Broadmeyer, you talk to Arnold. We'll compare notes later.'

'Awesome.'

Walking along the squishy sand and dodging in and out of the other surfers, I approached Tom with a beaming smile. I'm the face of *Click!*, so it's important to be friendly and professional.

'Tom? Tom Broadmeyer?' I asked.

He was brushing a towel across his wet head with one hand and carrying his board under his arm with the other. 'Yeah, that's right.'

'I'm—'

He stopped and then grinned. 'You're that newspaper girl… Stacey McLaren,' he said. 'I read that article you wrote on Fletcher.'

'Scoop. Scoop McLaren,' I corrected him. Then I held out my hand. 'Editor of *Click!*'

He shook it as he began walking again. 'Yeah, *Click!*. People have been talking about you. Surfers, I mean.'

'Really?' I asked, following behind him.

'Yeah. They all want to get in your paper, everybody is reading it, and well… I… wouldn't mind myself. You never know who might see the article. Trainers, sponsors… My dad says any publicity is good publicity.'

'Well, today is your lucky day,' I told him, ushering him to a bench just outside Mr Mack's café. 'My reporter, Evie, and I are compiling a list of competitor profiles and I'd love to include you.'

'For real?' he asked. 'Front page?'

'Well, sport is traditionally saved for the back pages, but if you actually go on to win the competition, I'm sure you'll make front page then.'

'Wicked!'

We sat down and I turned my voice recorder on. 'So, you fancy your chances then? Of winning the surfing competition of the year?'

'Is that thing on?' he asked, nodding towards the voice recorder. 'Am I being interviewed, like… right now? For real?'

'Yes.'

'Right.' For some strange reason he straightened his hair. Then he tilted his head to one side and thought for a moment. 'Well, yes. I mean, I do. Fancy my chances, that is. Of winning. The competition. Yes. Absolutely.'

'Right. What do you have that no other competitor here has?' I asked.

'Well, for starters, I've got my dad, ex-pro surfer, Ace Broadmeyer, as my coach. Have you ever heard of him?'

I shook my head. 'No, sorry.'

'He's a surfing legend back in Dandelion Beach. That's where we come from. He's won *heaps* of trophies. He says winning is everything,' he smiled.

'Is that so? And what do you think, Tom?' I leaned in, my voice recorder poised. '*Is* winning everything?'

'Well, it's pretty cool. Dad says winning is *really* important and that I must win, at all costs. He says that's why Broadmeyers surf – to be the best.'

Must win at all costs? Hmmm… very interesting!

He frowned as I jotted his quotes down in my notebook.

'Go on,' I said, holding the voice recorder closer.

'Actually… you better not put all that in the paper,' he said. 'I probably should have talked to Dad before I said anything.'

'That's all right,' I told him. 'It hasn't been uploaded yet. How about I just say that you're looking forward to the semi-final and that you rate your chances of winning as…?'

'Wicked good,' he nodded. 'Yeah, just put that. Dad says it's important to maintain a good image. I guess I just let my mouth run away with me sometimes,' he laughed.

'So, I guess your dad just wants you to be the best you can be, huh? Is he always encouraging you to be… *competitive*? Like at other tournaments you go to?'

'Yeah,' he shrugged. 'I guess.'

Awesome! We might have a suspect! I couldn't wait to tell Evie.

I looked around then back at Tom. 'Have you seen Fletcher?'

'You know In Flight pretty well?'

'Yes. He's staying with us.'

Tom got up and began drying his hair with his towel again. 'He's coming around to my place this afternoon, after lunch, to play video games. Well, the place we're staying at anyway. Mum and Dad have rented a house at the end of The Esplanade. You want to come?'

'Can I bring my friend, Evie?'

'Sure.'

♥

I couldn't see Evie anywhere on the beach, so I messaged her as soon as I got home to tell her I had my first suspect!

His dad sounds pretty full-on, I wrote. **He told Tom that he must win, AT ALL COSTS!**

Wow, that is full-on! she replied. **What now, boss?**

We're invited to his house this afternoon.

And?

While he and Fletcher are playing video games, you and I will have a look around. Maybe we can find some clues or evidence.

What about the paper? Are you going to write a story about our near miss?

No. If someone is out to get Fletcher it would be best for us to investigate under the radar.

Under the radar?

Yes. Quietly. Don't let them know we're on the case. If they think we're investigating, they'll probably tighten their tactics, make it harder for us to catch them.

Right!

What did you find out about Wallace Arnold?

Arghh! Nothing. He just kept answering my questions with 'yes' and 'no'. Nothing juicy or incriminating at all. But I also spoke to a boy called Daniel Wayland, 'The Wall'. That's a nickname he gave to himself by the way!

Oh, wow! And?

Well, I did some research and he's been rising strangely.

I've never heard of him.

Nobody has! And get this – he's not even interested in surfing! And he's not even that good.

Hmmm. How did he get into the semi-final then?

Good question.

♥

That afternoon, Evie skipped along The Esplanade as we made our way to the Broadmeyers' house. My Roving Reporter and I were still analysing things…

'Daniel admitted that he would actually rather be back being a holiday boarder at his boarding school in London,' she told me.

'Really? That's odd.'

'Exactly – totally weird. Then he started telling me all about his love for astronomy and how if I ever stepped on the moon, my footprints would remain there forever. Pretty awesome, huh?'

'Yes, but that doesn't help us. I still think we should keep an eye on our uncoordinated and uninterested surfer friend, Daniel Wayland, though. It could all be a clever act to throw the harbour's feisty detective editor—'

'You.'

'And her amazing roving reporter—'

'Me,' she beamed.

'Off track.'

'Great thinking, Scoop.'

'In the meantime, Tom is our *best* suspect to date.'

♥

At Tom's house, Mrs Broadmeyer had sliced up yummy watermelon for us and laid out big bowls of potato crisps. Her face was really quite round, and her cheeks glowed a rosy pink. She was super nice, called us all 'sweetums' and made us feel at home.

'Now, Scoop, tell me, dear, that's not your *real* name, is it?' she asked as we settled into the lounge.

'No, my real name is Henley. Henley Sarah McLaren. People just call me Scoop because I have my own online newspaper,' I told her.

'Ah, yes, Tom's very excited about your interview. Says he's going to be on the front page.'

'Oh, Mum, jeez!' Tom wailed from the floor. He and Fletcher were on their tummies in front of a huge TV screen, playing video games. 'I said I *might* be front page. I've got to win first.' Then he turned back to his game.

Mrs Broadmeyer smiled and gave me a wink. 'As if he *won't* win,' she said. 'He's been undefeated for the past eight months.'

'Really?' Evie asked.

'Yes. Now you two make yourselves comfortable. I'm sure the boys will let you have a turn soon.' She turned to Tom and Fletcher who were glued to the screen and gaming madly. 'Right, boys?' she called.

'Yeah, yeah, sure,' Tom said, not taking his eyes from the screen.

'Oh, we're fine,' I said. 'We're happy to wait our turn.' Then I plonked down onto the sofa and beckoned for Evie to join me.

'Well it could be a while,' Mrs Broadmeyer said, rolling her eyes. 'I'll be upstairs if you kids need me.' Then she was gone.

Evie leaned over and whispered, 'So? What now?'

'Um, boys? We're bored. We'll be off now,' I said.

'Ka-pow!' Tom yelled as he obliterated a slimy green alien. 'Take that!'

'Say, boys?' Evie said, smiling at me. 'I think the kitchen is on fire.'

'No, thanks,' Tom said. 'We're not hungry.'

'What about you, Fletch?' I called. 'We're flying to Paris. Want to come?'

'Nah,' he replied. 'I went before I got here.'

I shook my head. 'Numbskulls,' I told Evie. 'Come on, let's go!'

Evie followed me as I made my way through the kitchen and out of the back door.

The grass was high in the back yard, like it hadn't been mowed in months.

'What are we looking for?' Evie asked.

'Hopefully something that ties the Broadmeyers to our near miss last night,' I told her. 'Come on, follow me.'

As we waded our way through the long grass I looked around and soon spied an imposing wooden screen.

'We have the exact same screen at home,' Evie said, pointing. 'Dad uses it to cover up our compost heaps.'

'I wonder what the Broadmeyers are using it to cover

up?' I asked and Evie's eyes widened with curiosity.

We trudged on a bit further and peeked around the corner of the screen to find a tiny little outhouse with a ramshackle old door and a window. Paint was peeling from the walls and the door handle was broken. I marched towards it.

'Careful, Scoop,' Evie said. 'You never know what's inside there. Or *who*.'

When I pushed on the door it slowly opened and I peeked inside.

'See anything?' Evie asked. 'Any incriminating evidence?'

I sighed. 'No. Nothing but a bunch of old garden tools,' I replied. 'Let's push on.'

The yard was quite big, about twice the size of our yard at home. On the opposite side I saw a large, neglected vegetable garden over by the fence and a shed next to it. An out-of-control pumpkin vine had wiggled its way over the top.

Evie looked at me and grinned. 'This looks promising,' she said.

'Yes. Maybe we'll find a clue in there,' I told her. She nodded and followed me.

When we got to the shed, I peered through a crack in between the two rickety old doors.

'Jackpot,' I said with a smile.

'What is it?' Evie asked as she squinted into the darkness. 'I can't see anything at all.'

'It's a motorbike,' I told her.

She gasped and grabbed my arm. 'Like the one that tried to run us down?'

'I won't know unless I get a better look.'

Evie tugged on the padlock that hung on a chain to keep the doors closed and it opened very easily.

'Awesome!' she said. 'Tom's dad must've thought he locked it but didn't.'

She looked around before taking the lock off and pulling the chain through. The doors slowly crept open with a whiny creak and we stepped inside.

'Any idea where Tom's dad is?' Evie asked.

'Don't worry. Tom said he had to go into Cascade Point Shopping Centre to buy some special wax for his surfboard. He won't be back for ages.'

'Cool.'

We moved towards the bike. Even though it was broad daylight outside, it was a little dark inside the old shed. Our only light was a thin beam streaming through a small window at the side. The whole place smelled dreadfully musty and was littered with rubbish – old paint tins, rusty tools and Christmas decorations that had definitely seen better days. We carefully waded through the maze of garbage until we got to the motorbike.

'What do you think?' I asked Evie as we stood next to the bike. 'Look familiar?'

She sighed. 'I'm afraid I don't know. It happened so fast, and you got a better look than anyone.'

I examined the bike closely. I ran my hand over the chassis and felt something, a bump.

'There's a badge on here,' I told Evie. I whipped out my phone and turned on the torch. 'Bingo!' I cried.

'What?' Evie asked. 'What is it?'

Then I heard something. Outside. Someone... whistling. I tiptoed to the door and peered out.

'Oh no,' I whispered.

'Scoop! What's going on?' Evie cried.

I turned to face her. 'There's a man outside, probably Tom's dad. And he's heading straight for this shed!'

CHAPTER THREE

I pushed an old drum up to the shed door. I knew it wouldn't hold for long, but it was better than nothing.

'Yikes!' cried Evie, peering through the crack. 'Now he's talking to Mrs Broadmeyer, but he's pointing at the shed. Quick, we need to hide!'

Ace Broadmeyer was a big man and from first glance, he didn't look at all friendly. His arms were bulging with muscles and covered with tattoos of skulls and snake's heads, while on his fingers he wore an array of chunky silver rings.

'No, we don't need to hide, Evie, we need to get out!' I told her.

'But how do we get out? The only way out is through the door.'

I looked up. 'The window! It's only small but so are we. We'll fit.'

'How are we going to get up there?'

Quickly scanning the shed, I spied a small wooden table. I managed to drag it quite easily to underneath the window.

'Still too low, Scoop. We won't make it,' Evie said before peering outside. 'Hurry! Mrs Broadmeyer's going back inside and Mr Broadmeyer's just grabbed Tom's surfboard. I think he's bringing it in here to wax it!'

Heart pounding, I continued to look about. *An old trunk!*

'Quickly, Evie, help me lug this trunk on top.'

It wasn't as heavy as it looked, although it was heavy enough, but we managed to put it on top of the table.

'Fantastic!' Evie said.

'Quickly,' I whispered to my friend. 'Climb up and out!'

'What about you?'

'I'll be right behind you.'

Evie scaled the makeshift ladder with ease. Then she pulled open the window and shimmied through. I watched as her hands hung for a moment on the window ledge, then I heard her hit the grassy ground outside. To her credit, she didn't squeal!

'Hang about. I thought I locked this blasted shed,' said a voice.

It was Broadmeyer, at the door. I pulled my phone from my pocket, determined to get a quick picture of the badge on the bike, but when I pressed on the screen, it was black. *Darn! What a time for a dead battery!*

'Who's in there?' Broadmeyer bellowed. 'I can hear you! This is private property, you know. When I get my hands on you!' As he started pushing, the drum behind the door began swaying.

Shivering with fear, I made my way, firstly up the small table, then over the trunk. But just as I was about to go through the window, the trunk fell, toppling to the ground with a thud and leaving me dangling by my fingertips.

Broadmeyer pushed and the drum rocked. I knew it was only a matter of mere seconds before it tumbled over, leaving him with a free passage to enter.

With all the strength I could muster, I hoisted myself up and through the window. I could see Evie on the other side, beckoning for me to join her.

'Just fall through!' she loudly whispered. Then she ran to the corner of the shed and peered to get a location on Broadmeyer. 'Oh… *fudge*!' she said, running back. 'He's almost in! You need to get out, Scoop, and now!'

I was so scared, I froze. Not only was I dangling, like a seesaw, in the window, but I had Tom's irate dad almost on one side, and a pretty sharp fall awaiting me on the other.

'Right!' Broadmeyer said, pushing through. The drum went flying. 'Got it!' he cried as he entered. 'Now… what do we have here?'

With every fibre of my being I pushed forward and fell onto the grass below, the window closing shut behind me. I landed flat on my bottom! Evie pulled me to my feet.

'You okay, Scoop?' she asked.

'Yes,' I said, feeling around. *No sore spots!* 'I'm fine. Let's go!'

We ran to the back fence. It looked ancient, weathered by the sun, beaten by the rain, and, thankfully for us, every second picket was missing. We managed to climb through, one after the other. On the other side, we found ourselves on Seaside Drive, not far from my house.

'Evie, can I borrow your phone?' I asked.

'Sure,' she said, handing it to me.

I started typing.

'What are you doing?'

'Messaging Fletcher to tell him to get out of that

house and to come home super fast.'

Fletch, you have to get out of there! Pronto! Act cool though. Just say you forgot something and you have to leave. DO IT! Meet me at home. Scoop.

'But why? What's going on? What did you see on the bike, Scoop?' Evie asked frantically.

'I'll explain later. For now, we have to get out of here.'

Evie and I then linked hands… and ran all the way home.

♥

Dad wasn't home when we got there so I couldn't tell him what I had found out by sneaking into Broadmeyer's shed.

'It was a badge,' I told Evie as I made us a glass of chocolate-flavoured milk each. 'On the motorbike – it was a badge of an eagle!'

'Just like you thought you saw on the bike that almost knocked us over! It *was* Mr Broadmeyer,' she said, leaning over the kitchen counter.

'Exactly. He was probably trying to remove Fletcher

from the competition so Tom could win. Tom said his dad always told him that he must win, at all costs.'

'Do you think Tom knows? And Mrs Broadmeyer?'

'I'm not sure,' I said, handing Evie her milk and tossing a spoon into the sink. Then I plugged my phone in to recharge and sat down opposite her at the kitchen table.

'Hmm, yummy!' she said, taking a sip. 'My favourite! Where to now, Scoop?'

'We need to tell your dad, just as soon as he gets home from Dentons Grove Police Station. What time did you say that was?'

'Four o'clock. Their sergeant has come down with a cold, so Dad's been doing regular patrols to help out.'

'That gives us fifteen minutes to finish our milk and get down to your house. I wonder if Fletcher is on his way back now. I specifically said "pronto".'

'Boys!' Evie shook her head. 'They never do anything they're told.'

Just then Evie's phone chimed. 'It's Fletcher,' she said, handing it to me.

What are you on about, Scoop? I'm winning!

'Darn,' I said.

'What did he say?' Evie asked, stealing a peek at the screen.

'He's being annoyingly uncooperative!'

Is Mr Broadmeyer there? I answered back.

Dunno. Why?

Please, Fletch, just please come home now. You might be in danger. Hurry!

Minutes ticked away with no sign of Fletcher or any response to my last message.

'Strange he isn't answering,' Evie said, staring at her phone screen.

'Yes, and I'm worried. I'm going to phone my dad.'

'Good idea.'

I was just about to dial Dad's number when Evie's phone chimed again.

'It's Fletch,' I told her, reading the screen.

'Finally,' she sighed.

All right, all right. Mr Mack wants me to meet him at the surf shop café at four anyway. I'll leave now, he wrote.

Great! We'll meet you there. YFIS, DE.

Huh???

Sorry! Force of habit!

Huh???

Just get out, NOW!

'What's going on?' Evie asked.

'Fletcher's leaving now.'

'Thank goodness for that,' she said.

'Yes. I told him we'd meet him at the surf shop café. Your dad should be nearly home by now. Let's tell him everything we know then head to the café to meet Fletcher. I'll just write my dad a note to tell him where we are, and then we can go.'

Evie jumped up out of her chair and put her empty glass into the sink. 'Excellent milkshake, Scoop. You could put Mr Mack out of business,' she grinned.

♥

Sergeant Andrews said if he could indeed get a

look at the motorbike with the eagle badge on it in Broadmeyer's shed, teamed with my eyewitness account, he had good cause to bring Tom's dad in for questioning over the near miss that could've taken Fletcher out of the surfing competition.

He was on his way over to ask Broadmeyer a few questions when Evie and I met Fletcher at the surf shop café.

We found him outside with his head buried in his hands and looking totally bummed.

'What's up, Fletch?' I asked, plonking down next to him on the café steps.

'Yeah,' Evie said, joining us. 'Why the sour face?'

He sighed. 'Mr Mack can't train me any more; says he's got too much on his plate. More important things to worry about.'

'Oh. Well, that's not cool,' Evie said.

'But look on the bright side, Fletch,' I told him. 'You've still got my dad.'

'Yeah.' He smiled weakly. 'I do, and Uncle Ted's awesome and everything. It's just that... well, Mr Mack *was* a surfing champion. With him *and* Uncle Ted training me, I... I honestly thought I had the best chance of winning.'

I patted him on the back. 'You'll do fine, Fletch.

With or without Mr Mack, you're a champion.'

'Thanks, Scoop.'

'Besides, we've got big news.'

'*Huge* news,' Evie said, nudging him.

'About Tom Broadmeyer's dad.'

'He's a *huge* cheat.'

'He's most probably the one who tried to run us over last night.'

Fletcher was looking back and forth at us, like he was watching a tennis match. 'Wait, just… one at a time,' he said.

Evie rolled her eyes. 'Tom Broadmeyer's dad is a rotten, huge cheat and he's most probably the one who tried to run us down with his motorcycle last night!'

'For real?' Fletcher asked, his eyes wide.

'Yep,' I replied.

'Wow… so you were right?'

Evie laughed. 'When are you going to learn, Fletch? She's *always* right.'

I blushed. 'Evie,' I said. 'Not always.'

'Anyway,' she continued, 'my dad's out looking for him right now, and he's going to be in *so* much trouble.'

'Well… what about Tom?' Fletcher frowned. 'Do you think he knew?'

I shrugged. 'That's up to Sergeant Andrews to decide. I can't wait to find out though. This is going to be the best front page we've had in ages! Plus, you must be relieved, Fletch? To know the culprit's been caught. No more sabotage.'

'I guess,' he shrugged.

'Cheer up, Fletch,' Evie said, getting to her feet. 'Let's go inside and get some hot chips.'

We had just settled into a comfy booth by the door when Mr Mack sailed over to us.

'How come you don't want to train Fletcher any more?' Evie blurted out. 'What's he done wrong? Nothing, I bet. You're just being mean.'

'Evie!' I said and she turned away. I gave Mr Mack a little smile. 'Just three plates of hot chips please.'

He nodded. Then he turned to Fletcher, his dark brown eyes softening for a moment. 'It's… it's nothing personal, Fletcher,' he said. 'I've just got a lot to do at the moment, stuff that needs my full attention, that's all.'

Fletcher half smiled. 'That's okay. I've still got Uncle Ted,' he said. 'But, if I make it into the final, will you come and watch me surf?'

Mr Mack shrugged. 'If you make it into the final… I'll surely go on down and watch you surf,' he said.

Fletcher smiled. 'Thanks.'

'Hey, Mr Mack,' Evie beamed. 'Did you catch sight of the whales out in the ocean this morning? It was *A-MAZING!* My dad said he's never seen whales so close to the shore before.'

'No, I didn't, and in any case, I couldn't,' he mumbled. 'I'm short-sighted.' Then he turned to Evie. 'Happy?' he snapped.

Evie frowned and folded her arms. 'I was just trying to make conversation,' she quietly said. 'And they were amazing.'

I gave her a wink and a smile, and she brightened a little.

As Mr Mack sauntered back into the kitchen, I turned to my friends.

'I wonder what's going on with him?' I asked. 'He seems awfully cranky, I mean… crankier than usual, and worried about something.'

'*I* bet it has something to do with the man in the suit,' Evie quipped.

'Could be,' I replied. 'I think we should keep our eyes peeled. If he ever returns, we'll do some investigating.'

'Good idea, boss,' Evie said. She was making a house out of a napkin as we waited for our chips to arrive.

The sea breeze was gently blowing in through the front doors, trying to wisp away with Evie's napkin.

Fletcher gave a chuckle. 'You two,' he said, shaking his head. 'Isn't *one* mystery at a time enough for you to solve?'

Evie stopped with her house-making and looked over at Fletcher. 'You underestimate us, Fletch. We're super sleuths!' she cried. 'Right, Scoop?', and I proudly nodded in agreement.

'Well as long as you catch whoever is trying to keep me out of the competition, I'll be happy,' he said.

'Don't worry, Fletch, I'm almost certain Ace Broadmeyer is the culprit,' I told him. 'And now that Evie's dad is on the case, I don't think Broadmeyer will be bothering anyone any more.'

♥

After Fletcher went home, Evie and I sat on the beach, relaxed after a big day of sleuthing.

Evie's dad sent her a message to say that when he got to Broadmeyer's house, he was nowhere to be found, adding even more weight to our theory that he was behind the shenanigans to try and take Fletcher out of the competition.

'Scoop, I wanted to tell you about something… something rather strange that I discovered by doing research at the library,' Evie said.

'Research about what?'

'For my next article about the history of Higgity Harbour, when I came across a dusty old book that was neatly tucked away in the history section. It was all about the Dastardly Curse of Deadeye Dan.'

I sat forward and took my sunglasses off. 'The what?' I asked. I'd never heard of it before.

'It's a curse that the horrible pirate, Deadeye Dan Durnam, put on Higgity Harbour.' She leaned in close and her eyes went all squinty as she told the story. 'Legend has it that on his deathbed, still enraged at being beaten to the discovery of the town by Henry Higgity, Deadeye Dan swore to cause havoc, from beyond the grave, for Higgity Harbour whenever a full moon appears on the same night as the summer solstice.'

I frowned. 'When is that?'

'Well it's really, really rare,' she shrugged, as if it were a fact that everyone should know. 'But he vowed to make mayhem in the *days leading up to* and *on* the night.'

'Well, did you investigate further? When's the next

full moon due to appear on the same night as the summer solstice?' I asked.

She looked at me and gulped. 'On the eve of the Monster Wave final. Think about it, Scoop. It would explain all the strange things that are happening to Fletcher. And if the curse *is* real, the worst is yet to come!'

'Evie, do you really believe all this? That it's the work of a curse?' I asked my friend.

'I'm just putting it out there. I asked a few people, locals on Main Street, and most of them say it's nonsense, but a few people really and truly believe that…' she looked up into the sky, '… otherworldly forces may be at play here.'

'Well, I don't believe in curses,' I told her firmly. 'Dad always taught me to trust in the facts of the matter. I believe that Broadmeyer is behind all of this.'

'Suit yourself, boss,' Evie smiled. 'And if it turns out that Broadmeyer *is* the culprit, then we will have solved this mystery in record time,' she beamed. She took her cardigan that she had tied around her waist and draped it across her shoulders. It was starting to get cool out.

'Hey, you're right,' I smiled as we both gave ourselves a pat on the back. Then we giggled. Giggling is one of the best things I like to do with Evie!

I took out my trusty notebook. 'I think it's only a matter of time before your dad finds Broadmeyer and charges him for attempting to run Fletcher down. We had better be prepared to write the story up fast, so we don't get out-scooped by the metro papers. Let's go over a few possible headlines.'

'Right,' Evie said, concentration etched across her face. 'Hmm… a headline, a headline.'

I felt inside my pocket for my sparkly silver pen.

'Oh no,' I said.

'What's wrong?'

I turned my pocket inside out. *Nothing.* Then the other. *Nothing!*

'My sparkly pen – it's gone!' I told Evie.

'Are you sure you had it with you?'

'I never go anywhere without it!'

'Well, come on.' She jumped up. 'I'll help you look.'

Half an hour later and the light was fading. We had scoured every inch of the beach and found nothing.

'Oh, this is just *awful*,' I cried.

'Don't worry, Scoop. I'm sure it's at the surf café,' Evie said as we trudged towards the shop. 'It probably fell out of your pocket when we were eating chips in the booth.'

Mr Mack had closed up for the day and there wasn't another soul about.

We looked on the steps around the front of the shop and searched through the car park we had walked through earlier, but nothing. Evie even tried to peer through the surf café windows.

'It's kind of dark, but… I can't see it on the floor anywhere,' she said.

I sighed. 'You know what this means?'

'What?'

'Mr Mack probably found it on the floor and tossed it in with the rubbish. We're going to have to go through the garbage out the back. Sorry.'

'Okay,' Evie huffed, leading the way. 'But don't ever say I'm not a good friend.'

'You're the best,' I told her as we rounded the corner.

Searching through every rubbish bin at the back of the shop, we came across banana peels, empty crisp packets, sloppy pancake batter, half-eaten hot dogs and loads of other rubbish. But no pen.

Then Evie's phone dinged.

'It's my dad,' she said, checking the screen. 'He says we better go home, what with Broadmeyer still unaccounted for, he says it's not safe for us to be out this close to dark.'

'Okay,' I said softly. 'Sadly, it looks like my pen is gone anyway. Let's go.'

We brushed ourselves off and went to retrieve our backpacks.

'You never know, Scoop, it might turn up,' Evie said. 'Besides, everybody knows you own that pen. I'm sure it'll be returned. Like, remember the time you almost left it in the council car park when you were investigating the Mayor?' Then she laughed. 'You would've been in *so* much trouble had that horrible Ludwick found it. Heaven knows what he would've done if he found you spying—'

Her words stopped me in my tracks. 'Oh no. No, no, no,' I gulped.

'What? Don't worry about Mayor Ludwick now, Scoop. He's in prison! He can't hurt you.'

'It's not Mayor Ludwick that I'm worried about, Evie,' I said, turning to her. 'I had that pen when I was at the Broadmeyers' today. I think I must've dropped it in—'

'My shed,' a gruff voice said from behind us.

We turned around to find Ace Broadmeyer, holding my pen and standing between us and any possible escape route.

CHAPTER FOUR

Broadmeyer began circling us menacingly. Although he appeared cool and calm, his beady eyes were alive with rage.

'Here's your pen, *Scoop*,' he said, tossing it at my feet. 'I hear you're a pretty good detective editor. Perhaps you can shine some light on exactly *why* you were in my back shed today? And now I have the police after me. What do you make of that?'

'I… I guess Evie and I just got lost. We were playing video games, with Fletcher and Tom. That's all.'

I gulped down hard and very slowly put my hand in my pocket. From memory, I pushed a few buttons and hoped against hope that I had managed to press RECORD.

'You didn't tell Sergeant Andrews that you saw a motorcycle in the shed?'

'We didn't see anything,' I stammered. 'In your

shed, I mean. It was too dark. Right, Evie?'

'Yes, that's right. Certainly not a motorcycle. And most certainly *not* a motorcycle with an eagle badge on it.'

Oh, Evie!

'So, you *did* see it,' he whispered through gritted teeth. He stepped closer. 'You know. You know it was me who tried to run you down last night, don't you? You ran to the police and told them!'

I didn't respond. My heart was pounding fast, and my head felt light. So light that I was certain even a whimper of a breeze would blow me over.

'Well the bike's gone now,' Broadmeyer spat. 'I dumped it this afternoon, some place no one will ever find it. No evidence. Sergeant Andrews will never see it, so now it's just the word of two silly schoolgirls against mine.'

'So… you'll let us go now?' I asked. 'If we promise to say that we saw nothing? Like you said – there's no evidence. You outsmarted us. So… can we go?'

'Do I look stupid?' he asked.

'A little,' Evie said, and I motioned for her to stay silent.

'I can't take any chances. You two have no idea what's riding on my Tom winning these competitions,'

Broadmeyer said, moving in ever closer. 'No idea what I'm prepared to do to make my boy the best junior surfer this country has ever produced.'

He lunged at me and grabbed me by the scruff of my neck.

'No!' Evie cried. She bounced forward and, using her amazing karate skills, expertly snap-kicked Broadmeyer right in the knee.

Go, Evie!

'Owww!' he screamed, letting go of me and falling to the ground. But it didn't take him out fully. In fact, it just made him angrier! 'Why you...' He reached out with his long arm and grabbed Evie by the ankle. She squealed, and that's when I saw a man, stepping out from the shadows of the descending darkness. He had a big, heavy frying pan in his hands. I watched as he lifted it up before clocking Broadmeyer right over the head with it.

'Yay,' Evie squealed as Broadmeyer fell backwards. 'Mr Mack to the rescue!'

'All right, all right,' Mr Mack said as he leaned down to get a better look at Broadmeyer who was now off with the fairies. 'Looks like he'll be out long enough for the police to get here. You okay, Scoop?'

'Yes, thank you,' I replied, whipping out my phone.

'*And* I managed to record the entire conversation.'

'Good one!' Evie beamed. 'I'll call my dad.' She stepped aside, leaving Mr Mack and I to guard Broadmeyer.

'So, this is what you do, right?' Mr Mack asked me. 'Sneak around, solve puzzles and catch bad guys?'

'Yes,' I smiled. 'But not without a little help sometimes.' I reached out and Mr Mack shook my hand.

'It was nothing,' he said. 'You're just lucky I forgot to turn the alarm on when I left this afternoon. That's why I came back.'

'You know, Mr Mack, there's an app you can get on your phone that lets you turn the alarm off and on from wherever you are,' I told him as I pulled my jacket from my backpack and slipped it on.

'Nah, I don't go in for all that silly technology mumbo-jumbo,' he said. 'I'm what you kids call a… a… Luddite?'

'Oh, er… right,' I said.

Mental note: google 'Luddite'.

'I wouldn't know a smartphone from a…'

'Tablet?' I offered.

'Whatever,' he said. Then he leaned down and picked up his frying pan. 'Besides, if I had that silly app, I never would have come back here and saved you and Evie, now would I?'

'I suppose,' I replied. 'Thanks again for that. It was much appreciated,' I smiled.

'No one knows this about me, but I always wanted to be a policeman,' he said.

'Well I think you'd make a very good one!'

♥

Sergeant Andrews arrived a few minutes later. He was pleased to have his prime suspect captured.

'Good work, Juniper,' he said to Mr Mack as a young constable bundled a now conscious Broadmeyer into the back of a police car.

Evie and I turned to each other. '*Juniper?*' we said.

'Like I said to Scoop, it was nothing,' Mr Mack frowned. 'Nothing anyone else wouldn't have done, so… just forget it.' He quickly marched into the back of the shop and was gone.

Just then my dad and Fletcher appeared from around the corner of the shop. Dad ran up to me and grabbed me in a hug. 'Are you okay, sweetheart?' he said, squeezing me tightly. 'Sergeant Andrews told me everything.'

'Yes, Dad, I'm fine. The police have our suspect and I have a taped confession, of sorts. Enough all round to pin all this on Broadmeyer, I would say.'

'Thank goodness,' Dad replied, at last letting me go. 'Perhaps now we can relax and concentrate on the rest of the tournament?'

'Yes,' I beamed.

'Case closed,' Evie said.

Fletcher grabbed my arm and smiled. 'Thanks, Scoop,' he said.

I shrugged. 'It's just what I do,' I told him.

Sergeant Andrews walked over to us. He had his hands on his hips and his stern policeman face on. 'Although I specifically told you two that there was to be *no* investigating, and while I don't condone you girls skulking around deserted beaches close to dark, I will say… good work today,' he said, throwing an arm around Evie. 'I did a lot of sleuthing myself today and as it turns out, Broadmeyer has been causing quite a bit of attention since his arrival yesterday afternoon.'

'What do you mean?' Dad asked.

'He's also a suspect in a fuel theft down the road at Maitland's Mechanical Repair,' he huffed. 'You'd think for a criminal he'd be trying to keep a *bit* of a low profile.'

'Do you think his wife and son were in on it?' Dad asked.

Sergeant Andrews shook his head. 'Didn't have a clue. They're actually pretty devastated. Young Tom's pulled out of the competition and they're on their way home to Dandelion Beach as we speak.'

'That's a shame,' Dad said.

I stepped forward. 'So, Broadmeyer didn't arrive in Higgity Harbour until yesterday afternoon?' I asked.

'Yes, that's right,' Sergeant Andrews nodded.

'Hmm.'

'What, Scoop?' Dad asked.

I turned to my friend. 'Fletcher, tell me again when you *first* noticed that someone had been messing about with the time on your phone?'

'Um, let's see. The day before yesterday, as soon as I got out of the surf.'

'Oh dear,' I said.

'What?' Fletcher asked.

'Broadmeyer tried to take you out of the competition, yes, but if he didn't arrive in Higgity Harbour until yesterday afternoon and someone sabotaged the time on your phone before he even got here—'

'Then Broadmeyer isn't the only one trying to keep

Fletcher out of the competition!' Evie cried.

'That's correct, my roving reporter!'

HERO SHOPKEEPER SAVES LOCAL SUPER SLEUTHS

By Scoop McLaren

A Higgity Harbour business owner, who prefers to remain anonymous, has saved *Click!*'s very own editor, Scoop McLaren, and reporter, Evie Andrews, after the pair were accosted by Ace Broadmeyer, who police will allege tried to run down surfer, Fletcher Stein, in Higgity Harbour last night.

Police suspect that Broadmeyer planned to run down Fletcher in a bid to take him out of the Monster Wave Supreme Grommet Title, paving the way for his own son to win the prestigious tournament.

Competition officials were outraged to learn of the incident.

'The Legion of Preposterously Professional Surfers will not tolerate bad sportsmanship and absolutely forbid the partaking in illegal behaviour in order for surfers to get ahead in the competition,' the Legion's National President and head judge of the competition,

Hal Spinkman, told *Click!*.

'We pride ourselves on running a preposterously professional competition. May the best surfer win.'

Meanwhile, a huge crowd is expected to descend upon Higgity Harbour's Five-Mile Beach tomorrow, as young surfers from across the country and beyond battle it out for a place in Saturday's final.

♥

Fortunately for Fletcher, the sabotage attempts ceased, leaving him to concentrate on winning the semi-final, but that didn't stop Evie and I from reopening our investigation!

On the morning of the semi-final we took to the sand, discreetly asking questions to other competitors, trying to figure out the good sports from the potentially ruthless surfers who would stop at nothing to win.

After we finished our sleuthing, we plonked ourselves down onto the sand. 'Well, the only suspects on the list are Daniel Wayland and Charlie Perry, 'Wipe Out',' Evie went. 'Charlie said if he doesn't win the competition, his dad has threatened to get rid of his bike, scooter, laptop and all his fishing gear.'

'That's awful!' I said. 'Boy, these parents sure take

this surfing stuff seriously.'

'You can say that again. Anyway, that's all I have.'

'I spoke to the others. They were more interested in getting on the front page of *Click!* than they were about answering proper questions,' I sighed. 'At this stage, it could be anyone.'

'Or any*thing*,' Evie quipped as she kicked the sand. 'It could be the curse?'

I rolled my eyes. 'Curses aren't real, Evie.'

We found Fletcher outside the surf café, getting some last-minute tips from Dad. Mr Mack was there too but he didn't seem at all interested. He was too busy emptying grotty garbage bins.

Spectators began traipsing past us to claim good spots on the beach, perfect for viewing all the semi-final action.

Sabotage suspects aside, not only was I there to cheer Fletcher on and enjoy the competition, but I was also working on my paper. The surfing competition was the story on everybody's lips, and I was determined to give my readers the best coverage I possibly could.

'Just remember, Fletch, stay calm and do what comes naturally,' Dad said, smiling. 'You're easily the most dominant surfer out there. You're a natural!'

'Okay, Uncle Ted.'

'And don't forget – when you spot the wave, commit to it. It's all about confidence.'

'Sure thing,' Fletcher said. 'Got it. Stay calm, do what comes naturally… spot a wave and… then commit to it.'

Dad smiled and nodded.

'Come on, everyone, we better get down to the beach,' he said.

As we headed off, I heard a man's voice behind us. 'Juniper Mack?' he called.

I turned to see the man with the fancy suit and the shiny shoes, standing in the car park next to his sparkling sports car. He had his arms folded and was tapping his foot impatiently. Then I looked over at Mr Mack who was now quietly sweeping the pavement outside the surf café. His face had lost all colour and he gulped down hard at the sight of the man.

As Fletcher and Evie chatted excitedly about the prospect of Fletcher making it into the final, I walked backwards along the sand, watching Mr Mack as he had a conversation with the stern suit man. He had his hands out, as if pleading for reason, but the man just shook his finger in Mr Mack's face before he got into his car and drove off.

I took my camera out and zoomed in on the car's

licence plate – HMH-001.

Snap!

♥

There were people everywhere on the beach, armed with deckchairs, hats and sunscreen, all ready for the semi-final to begin.

Dad's number one sports journo, Kenny Dixon, was there with notebook in hand and one of Dad's cameras swinging around his neck.

'Hey, Scoop, Evie, Mr McLaren,' Kenny said, jogging up to us. 'How cool is this? The surf looks wicked and there are people everywhere!'

'All set, son?' Dad asked.

'Sure am! This is the biggest sports story I've covered to date. I'm hoping to get an exclusive with the win—' Then he stopped, looked at me and said with a chuckle, 'Scoop McLaren, let's see who gets in first!' Kenny always teases me. I giggled and Evie rolled her eyes at him.

'Would all competitors please take their places for the semi-final,' rang out a voice on the PA system.

'Okay, Fletch,' I said. 'This is it, good luck!'

'Thanks, Scoop,' he smiled as he ran to the

starting line.

The atmosphere on the beach was electrifying. Everyone from senior citizens to small children were glued to the sand, ready for all the excitement of the competition to unfold.

We all listened as a marshal explained the rules.

'Just like heats, semi-finals are ten minutes in duration,' he said. 'You start from the beach in an area designated for each bank. When the green flag is raised and the siren blasts, the competition has started. The judges will give between zero and ten points for each ride based on your performance. Your best two waves are counted for the total of your score from the judges. The first and second place competitors will progress to surf in Saturday's final.'

The marshal's voice trailed off as my attention turned to Evie who was nudging me in the ribs.

'Watch this,' she said, then winked.

She stood next to two of the semi-finalists. They were huge surfers who dwarfed Fletcher, Wallace and Daniel.

'Pssst,' she said to get their attention, and they looked over at her. 'You two are from Holland, right?' she asked.

They both nodded.

'Okay, take notes,' she continued. 'Fletcher Stein *owns* this beach. He's been surfing here since he was three. If he wins this competition, they're probably going to name a pier or something after him, so... I think you boys may as well just get back on the plane now. But thanks for coming.'

The big one turned to the slightly smaller one and laughed. 'Wie be dit weinig domkop?' he said.

I typed his response into the language app on my phone.

TRANSLATION: Who is this little dweeb?

The smaller one shrugged. 'Dom weinig jongen ziim poging aan merk ons nerveus.'

TRANSLATION: Stupid little idiot is trying to make us nervous.

Evie looked at them both with confusion as they burst out laughing and pointed at her.

She was very put out. She frowned. 'What did I say that was so funny?' she asked me.

I patted her on the back. 'Nice try, Evie, nice try.'

But Fletcher didn't need *any* help winning.

'Competitors ready! Good luck, surfers!' the marshal called, and with one big blast of the siren they were off!

We watched as the competitors ran into the surf with their boards. Fletcher was first in, with two others not far behind. The very last surfer to hit the water was Daniel Wayland.

With Evie jumping up and down and squealing beside me, I watched as Fletcher threw his board into the water and paddled out through the foam. Then he was up, on his board, gliding gracefully across the lip of a wave.

'That's it, Fletch,' I heard Dad call out. 'Commit to the wave!'

Fletcher carved the wave, up and down, as fellow surfers fell, one by one, around him.

Dad looked over at me. 'He's doing good,' he smiled. 'He's doing really, really good!'

I watched as Daniel Wayland climbed a wave, only to fall face first into the water, his gangly arms and legs everywhere.

When the first ride was over, the competitors made their way onto the shore with their boards. Some looked pleased with their performances, others disappointed, but Fletcher was grinning from ear to ear.

He raced over to us, and Evie and I gave him a thumbs-up. *Job well done!*

'How do you think I went, Uncle Ted?' he asked.

Dad scruffed Fletcher's hair. 'You did awesome!' he cried. 'You can count yourself into that final, son, I just know it!'

To all our delights, Fletcher performed even better in the second and final round of the semi-final.

Evie was positioned as close to the edge as she could possibly get to zoom in and capture action shots of Fletcher, mid-surf. The siren blared, signalling the end of the competition, and Evie jogged over to me with a happy look on her face.

'I managed to get some top shots, Scoop,' she said. 'Front page material for sure!'

'Great work,' I told her.

As the crowd settled around the scoreboard, eagerly awaiting the results, we walked over to the judges' table. The four judges, including National President, Hal Spinkman, were huddled in conversation until Mr Spinkman gave the marshal a nod to indicate that the final results were in. The marshal gave the judges a thumbs-up as he took a card from Mr Spinkman and walked up to the microphone on the podium.

'Okay, everyone, the results are in and it's time to

announce our winners,' he said.

'This is it, Fletch,' I heard Evie say. 'This is it!'

The crowd quietened down as the marshal read from the card. 'The winners of today's semi-final, taking a place in the grand final to compete for the championship are…'

'Wallace Arnold… and Daniel Wayland!' the marshal cried.

A stunned hush fell over the crowd as spectators stared at each other in disbelief. *Daniel was pitiful out there!*

'Woo hoo!' Wallace cried, knowing full well that Daniel would be a cinch to smash in Saturday's final. Unlike Fletcher, but he was now well and truly out of the race.

'Come on up here, boys,' the marshal said to Daniel and Wallace as a few lonely claps rang out.

As Daniel stumbled up onto the podium, I noticed the air around me was filled with bewildered whispers.

How on earth did he win?

I can't believe it – he was simply frightful!

Are the judges blind? Fletcher was much, much better!

Tiffany Tidwell, she's a girl in year 10, had actually fainted from the shock! A bunch of concerned onlookers swarmed around her until some nearby medics took over.

'Congratulations, honey bun!' Daniel's mum, Doris, yelled from the crowd. 'That's my boy!'

I looked over at my dad. He had his mouth open, but no words were coming out.

He was speechless!

We watched as Daniel took the card from the marshal. He pulled it up close to his face, as if to make sure that it was actually his name on it. He grinned widely. 'Wow,' he said. 'I won. I won!'

The gloomy crowd began to slowly disperse, and I saw quite a few people walk up to Fletcher with their heads shaking.

'I sure didn't see that coming,' Evie said as she skipped up beside me. 'How about you, Scoop? What do you think?'

I shook my head. 'Something's not right here,' I told her, 'and I intend to find out exactly what it is.'

When Daniel jumped down from the podium, I ran over to him. 'Daniel? Scoop McLaren from *Click!*,' I said. 'How do you think you went today? I mean, you just beat Fletcher Stein, who arguably just had his best surf in this competition. Yet, he's not in the final and you are? How do you explain that, Daniel?'

'Oh, um… well…'

Just then Kenny bounded over. 'Daniel,' he said. 'Kenny Dixon from the *Gazette*.'

As Kenny fired questions at Daniel, thick and fast, I looked over at Fletcher. Even though my dad was there to console him, he looked as if he'd lost his very last friend. I felt so sad for him but had to go interview the winners.

I pulled out my voice recorder. 'Daniel? You didn't answer my question,' I put to him. 'How *did* you beat Fletcher today? What do you put it down to? Your skill? Luck? Something... else?'

Kenny leaned over. 'Great questions, Scoop!'

'Daniel?' I continued. '*Can* you explain how you won?'

He swallowed down hard as I held my voice recorder up close to his face. 'Well,' he croaked, 'um... I guess...'

'That's quite enough, young lady.' His mother appeared, getting in between me and Daniel. 'You too,' she said to Kenny. 'No more interviews.'

'But, Mum,' Daniel protested, 'she's Scoop McLaren, from *Click!*. All the surfers want to be in *Click!*.'

'Daniel!' I cried, sidestepping his mum. 'They're all saying you don't deserve to win. What do you say about that? What do you say to all those people?'

'He doesn't say anything,' Mrs Wayland screeched before forcefully taking Daniel by the shoulders and turning him around.

'Daniel?' I asked. 'Your last chance to set the record straight?'

He looked at his mother and then managed to utter two words before being marched off, the two words that no detective editor ever wants to hear.

'No comment,' he said.

CHAPTER FIVE

UNKNOWN GROMMET SHOCKS HIS WAY INTO SURF FINAL

By Scoop McLaren

The local surfing fraternity is in a state of complete and utter disbelief with the defeat of Monster Wave surfing favourite, Fletcher Stein, 'In Flight', in today's action-packed semi-final at Five-Mile Beach.

Relatively unknown surfer, Daniel Wayland, who had what some surfing experts are describing as a 'disastrous set', was named a winner, securing himself a place in Saturday's final against Wallace Arnold.

Wayland was at a loss to explain his surprise win when approached by *Click!* after the semi-final. This editor would even go so far as to say that the boy was 'gagged' by his mother, who hurriedly rushed Wayland away, leaving local media and competition onlookers stunned with the realisation that the boy who almost drowned in the first round of the competition is now set to line up in the final.

With Stein out of the competition, commentators are predicting Wallace Arnold will walk away with the title.

The competition has so far been filled with controversy, with a former competitor's father in custody after attempting to run down Stein, and now Stein's shock exit.

STUNNED STEIN SPEECHLESS FOLLOWING SURF COMP EXIT

By Kenny Dixon

Stunned onlookers are not the only ones scratching their heads in confusion after surfing sensation Fletcher Stein was knocked out of the Monster Wave Supreme Grommet Title.

Stein, who was favourite to win the competition and who had a cracking set in the semi, said there wasn't much more he could have done to impress judges while carving up the surf at Five-Mile Beach.

'I don't know where I went wrong,' he told the *Gazette* after the semi-final. 'I really thought I had one of my best surfs ever.'

Stein, who is trained by the *Gazette*'s own surfing stalwart, Ted McLaren, thanked McLaren for all the training and support.

'I couldn't have gotten this far without him,' he said. 'Or Juniper Mack. He helped me at the start of the tournament as well.

'I guess it just wasn't my day.'

♥

'Well, at least I can stop worrying about whoever it is trying to take me out of the competition,' Fletcher said as the four of us sat in a booth at the surf shop café. 'I took myself out!'

'I still can't believe you didn't win, Fletch,' Kenny said, shaking his head. 'You were dead set the best surfer out there.'

'By far,' Evie chimed. She was sipping on a milkshake. Then she smiled at him sympathetically which I think he appreciated.

'Thanks, guys,' he said, playing with the top of his soda bottle. 'But I just want to forget about the surfing title now and enjoy the rest of my summer holiday.'

He flicked the soda top and it landed at Mr Mack's feet as he shuffled past the booth, sweeping. 'What do you think, Mr Mack?' Kenny asked, turning to him. 'Fletcher was the best out there today, right?'

He smiled. 'I didn't actually have a chance to get down to the beach today but I'm sure you really were the best, Fletcher,' he said, patting him on the back. 'So, chin up. There's always next time. Right, kids?'

He stared around at us, at our bewildered faces. I tried not to stare, Dad says it's not polite, but it was just that… I don't think I've ever seen Mr Mack smile! The skin around his eyes went all wrinkly and his whole face took on a strange, warm glow.

'Wow,' Evie said, the straw from her milkshake stuck to her bottom lip. 'You… you have teeth!'

He chuckled. 'I'm just saying, there'll be other competitions, son. It's not the end of the world. Now I'll be out back if you kids need anything else. Cheerio.' Then he was gone.

'Is it my imagination or was that *totally* weird?' Kenny asked.

'*Totally*,' Evie replied.

'Maybe he's just in a good mood?' Fletcher offered.

'In all those days he coached you, Fletch, was he

ever in a good mood?' Kenny asked.

Fletcher thought for a moment. 'Well… no, but I guess there's a first time for everything.'

♥

That afternoon Fletcher, Evie and I went and hung out in the town square. I suggested a movie to take Fletcher's mind off things, but he refused. Almost every resident who walked past us stopped to tell Fletcher how sorry they were not to be seeing him in the Monster Wave final.

To be honest, Daniel's win still didn't sit well with me and I could feel a funny feeling coming on.

'I've never left a mystery unsolved,' I told them as we lay on the lush green lawn under the Henry Higgity statue, 'and I'm not about to start now!'

'But now that Fletcher is out of the competition, we'll never know who the second saboteur was,' Evie said. Then she frowned. 'Um… I mean the *first*.'

'Just give up, Scoop,' Fletcher said, disheartened. He had his eyes closed and his face towards the sun. 'It doesn't matter now anyway. I'm out and that's that.'

'But I bet if we keep digging, we'll be able to figure it out,' I said as I sat up. I took out my notebook and my sparkly silver pen from my backpack. 'Now, Fletch, do you recall seeing anyone or anything out of the ordinary on the beach on the mornings your phone was tampered with?'

He sighed. 'You've asked me this before,' he said, 'and my answer is still the same – no. Just a bunch of surfers either catching a break or, like me, practising for the competition.'

'Hmm.'

'Except…'

'Except what?' I asked.

He sat up. 'Except that one morning when I saw Mr Spinkman.'

'The National President? So?'

'Well, he was standing in the car park, next to the surf shop café. But when he saw me, he turned and took off, like… like he didn't want me to know he was there. I guess I thought it was strange at the time, but… with everything going on, I just forgot to tell you.'

'What do you think, Scoop?' Evie asked.

'Well… I guess that is weird behaviour. Why would the National President be skulking around, not wanting to be seen? Unless…'

'Unless what?' Fletcher asked.

'Unless he was meeting with someone.'

'Another surfer?' Evie asked. 'Perhaps… to plan Fletcher's demise?'

'It's certainly a possibility,' I said as I scribbled SUSPECTS at the top of the page. Then I wrote *Hal Spinkman*. 'Okay, motive?'

'What's a motive?' Fletcher asked.

'The reason *why* someone does what they do,' Evie told him. 'In this instance, *why* would Spinkman want you out of the competition?'

'No idea. In fact, the better the surfers, the more exposure for the competition, and the Legion itself,' Fletcher said.

I huffed with frustration. 'Then it has to be something more important to him than the competition. But what?' I got up and started walking back and forth as I racked my brain for an answer.

'What's she doing?' Fletcher asked Evie.

'Oh, she's just pacing. It helps her think. She gets it from her dad. He's a pacer too!'

He stifled a laugh. 'She looks so serious,' I heard him whisper to Evie.

'That's because sleuthing *is* serious,' she replied, and I smiled. 'Most of the time anyway.'

I looked up and spied Imogen Blaxland, walking

across the square, making her way towards us.

'Oh, great,' Evie said. 'Just when I thought this day couldn't get any worse.'

'Who is it?' Fletcher asked.

'Imogen Blaxland. The nastiest girl in school. Disregard anything that she says, Fletcher. She's positively awful.'

'Well, well, well,' Imogen said as she parked herself down next to Evie on the grass. 'Fancy meeting you lot here.' She brushed a wayward black curl from her forehead and took the pink laptop she'd been carrying out from under her arm.

I really thought Imogen would be a bit nicer these days considering it was me who helped her out after Sonny Fink wrote that disastrous story about her.

'Oh, hi, Imogen,' I said.

'Hi, Henley.'

Then she flipped open her laptop.

'We all call her Scoop,' Evie spat, 'and since she saved you from sitting in stone for the rest of your life, the least you could do is call her Scoop too.'

'Sitting in stone?' Fletcher asked, frowning.

'It's a long story,' Evie told him.

'What are you up to, Imogen?' I asked her.

'Researching my family tree. My dad just bought

me this really cool software. You just type in your surname and it traces your ancestors.'

'Who cares about that sort of thing anyway?' Evie said.

'*I* do,' Imogen replied. 'I just *know* I'm related to royalty and this is going to help me prove it.'

'Whatever,' Evie quipped.

'That actually sounds pretty cool,' Fletcher piped up. 'Being related to royalty, I mean.'

Imogen looked over at Fletcher and smiled. 'Oh, Henley?' she said, not taking her eyes off Fletcher. 'Aren't you going to introduce me to your friend?'

I sighed. 'Imogen, Fletcher, Fletcher, Imogen. There. You're introduced.'

'Au shon tay,' Imogen said, shaking Fletcher's hand.
Mental note: google 'au shon tay'.

'If you actually don't mind, Imogen,' I said, 'we were in the middle of a very important—'

'Would you like a try?' she asked Fletcher, jumping over Evie and positioning herself firmly in between them. 'Do you know anything about your family history?'

'Well—'

'I wouldn't be surprised if you were related to royalty,' she gushed. 'What with your rugged good looks, there must be princely blood in you somewhere.'

Evie fell back onto the lawn and stuck her finger down her throat, pretending to gag.

Fletcher blushed. 'Oh, no,' he said. 'It won't work with me.'

Evie sat back up. 'Why not?' she asked.

'You see, my dad is adopted. He was in an orphanage until he was five. Then he got adopted by my grandparents.'

'Hmm,' Imogen said. 'Well, what about your mother? Was she a poor little orphan too?'

'Imogen!' I scolded. 'That's not very nice.'

'What?'

'My mum's maiden name is Stone. Felicity Stone,' Fletcher said.

Evie rolled over onto her tummy. 'You remember stone, don't you, Imogen? It's what Scoop saved you from remaining like for all eternity?'

'Stone,' she said as she typed it in, ignoring Evie. 'Right. It says here that the surname Stone is English.' With that, she slammed her laptop shut. 'So, you, dear Fletcher, are half English and half orphan.'

'Imogen!' I cried.

'What?' And she walked off.

♥

That night as I helped Dad do the dishes, I asked him about the Dastardly Curse of Deadeye Dan that Evie had told me about.

'Ah, yes,' he said as he scrubbed a plate clean. 'I'd almost forgotten about that.'

'So, you know about it?'

'Only what I've read in history books,' he replied.

'Evie said it happens when the full moon occurs on the same night as the summer solstice. Do you think it's real, Dad?' I asked as I carefully placed the cups I was drying into a cupboard. 'Do you think everything that's been going on lately could be because of Deadeye Dan's curse?'

'It all seems a bit silly to me, love,' Dad said. 'But then again, if Sonny Fink can write the news and then make it happen, I guess anything is possible?'

'I guess,' I shrugged. 'Evie says that pirates were usually very familiar with astronomy, that it helped them sail the seas.'

'That's true.'

'So, she believes it makes sense for Deadeye Dan to know a lot about the moon and the summer solstice.'

Dad stopped what he was doing and turned

towards me. 'Well, I… I guess it would.'

I put the last of the dry dishes in the dish rack. 'Evie is quite convinced. The next full moon due to appear on the same night as the summer solstice is on the night of the Monster Wave final. She thinks something terrible is going to happen!'

Dad rested his hand on my shoulder. 'I wouldn't worry too much, sweetie,' he said. 'Deadeye Dan also said that whoever looks at his grave at the stroke of midnight will turn to dust and that hasn't happened yet.'

'Have you ever, Dad? Looked at Deadeye Dan's grave at midnight?'

'Well, no, but…'

I leaned over the counter at him. 'Would you?' I asked.

'I think it's time you went to bed,' he replied, and he kissed my forehead.

'Right,' I nodded.

♥

The next day, I put the curse of Deadeye Dan out of my mind and arranged to interview Hal Spinkman in the members' area of the Higgity Harbour Surf Life

Saving Club, as a matter of urgency.

I told him I was doing an exclusive on the popularity of the competition, but I was more interested in him and any possible connection he had to this mystery.

He met me out the front on the pavement at precisely 2 p.m. Hal Spinkman was a tall, thin, lanky man with a wave of thick grey hair and a peculiarly long, pointy nose. As far as first impressions go, he didn't make a good one. I found him to be quite unfriendly – I don't think he smiled once – and he made it very clear that our interview would have to be short as he had 'more important things to take care of.'

However, I was used to how wary people could be around me, the newspaper girl. They were scared of perhaps saying the wrong thing and then having it plastered in black and white for all to see. *Especially* people who had something to hide.

'*Every* young surfer on the continent wants to win the Monster Wave Supreme Grommet Title,' Mr Spinkman proudly announced as we sat inside the club under the cool of a ceiling fan. He had secured a table with an ocean view and offered me fruit from a silver platter. 'That's the reason why we can offer so much in prize money. Sponsors are simply lining up to have their names associated with the competition.'

'I see,' I said, jotting notes down into my book.

'I created the competition three years ago,' he continued. 'We take it around, choosing little seaside towns just like Higgity Harbour to host it each season. It brings in competitors and fans from all over. A wonderful boost to the local economy.' Then he leaned over and banged a pointed finger down three times on my notebook. 'Make sure you put that in,' he said.

'Yes... Can I ask, Mr Spinkman, were you at all surprised by the result in the semi-final? I mean, nothing against Daniel Wayland, but Fletcher Stein had a near perfect set, and Daniel, well...'

He glared across the table at me and his eyes turned all squinty. 'I can't talk about that, about the judging process. The Legion forbids it. However, I will say that Daniel won, fair and square,' he said.

'I never said that he didn't... win fair and square, that is. I just said that his win was rather... surprising.'

I watched as Mr Spinkman pursed his lips and went a funny colour – kind of grey, mixed with yellow, mixed with green. Then he looked at his watch. 'I'm afraid this interview will have to be terminated,' he said, rising from his seat.

'Terminated? But…?'

'I must bid you good day, Miss McLaren. If you want to know anything else about the tournament for your story, Leo Levine, the vice president, will be able to help you.'

I stood up. 'But, Mr Spinkman…?'

'Good day.'

I watched as he hurriedly headed out of the front entrance. I jumped to my feet and quickly followed him.

Outside the Surf Life Saving Club, he raced down the stairs as fast as his spindly legs could carry him.

'Mr Spinkman!' I called after him. 'Just one more question, sir!'

As he sailed off the bottom step, I saw a little white card fall from his pocket. I hung back a second until he got into his yellow sports car and I watched him screech off. Once he was out of sight, I ran and picked up the card.

Just then I felt my phone vibrating in my pocket. It was a message from Evie.

Hey DE! How'd it go with Spinkman?

Hey RR! He got awfully nervous when I mentioned

Daniel winning. He said he won 'fair and square'. Why would he say that?

Hmmm... strange choice of words! I think he'd probably only say that if he knew Daniel DIDN'T win 'fair and square'.

Exactly! Then he got all funny and rushed off. Couldn't wait to get away from me!

He knows you're on to him! Keep sleuthing!

Hang on a sec, RR, I think he's left a clue!

It was a business card, engraved with silver lettering. It belonged to: HAL SPINKMAN, NATIONAL PRESIDENT OF THE LEGION OF PREPOSTEROUSLY PROFESSIONAL SURFERS. I turned it over, and in perfectly written handwriting was:

LPO 3.30 P.M. SHARP!!!

My phone chimed again.

DE? You still there?

Yes, and there's been a development in the case. I have a lead!

Awesome!

Looks like he's supposed to meet someone at 3.30 p.m.... sharp!

But where?

Doesn't exactly say, just... LPO. What could that mean?

Hmmm... Maybe it's the initials of the person he is to meet up with?

Maybe. But I'm thinking it's probably a nearby location. What could it be?

I brushed my hair from my eyes and thought for a moment.

Then my phone dinged once more.

I've got it, DE! Evie wrote. **Lightning Point Observatory!**

Excellent, RR! Let's meet at the old observatory in

fifteen minutes then. But take the short cut! YFIS, DE.

Right! See you then, YFIS, RR.

♥

True to form, my roving reporter met me at the foot of the old observatory at precisely 3.25 p.m. By taking the short cut through the scrub of Acacia Park, it meant we couldn't be seen by passing motorists, *specifically* Hal Spinkman.

We secured our hiding place behind a row of neatly trimmed lavender bushes and waited for Spinkman to arrive.

'Got your video ready?' Evie asked.

'Yes. All set. Something's going on here, Evie, I just know it.'

'If you say so, Scoop,' she said, giving me a thumbs up.

The whir of a car engine cut through the gentle humming of the ocean breeze, and Evie and I peered through the hedge as a bright yellow convertible drove up and parked next to the observatory.

'That's Hal Spinkman's car,' Evie said in a soft voice. 'I'd know it anywhere.'

Then a second car pulled in behind him. I whipped out my phone and began to video the scene.

We watched as Spinkman got out of his car and looked around before walking to the other vehicle. The second car's door opened and out stepped…

'That's Doris Wayland,' Evie whispered. 'Daniel's mother!'

'So it is.'

They shook hands and started talking.

'What are they saying?' Evie asked. 'I can't hear.'

'This is no good. We need to get closer,' I told her. 'I need to pick up sound. Come on.'

Evie followed me and we waddled, like ducks, behind the lavender hedge, edging closer to Spinkman and Mrs Wayland on the other side.

'How's this?' Evie asked.

'Spot on!' I replied.

But in the rush to get to the observatory, I forgot to turn down the volume on my phone, and it chimed.

Oh no!

Evie grabbed my arm and quietly gasped as I hit the mute button, but it was too late. We watched as Spinkman turned around to look in our direction.

'Hold on,' he said to Mrs Wayland, lowering down his voice. 'I don't think we're alone.'

Evie and I crouched down even further as he slowly creeped towards the lavender hedge.

'Anyone there?' he asked.

We held our breaths. Then I made my right hand into a fist and banged it twice on my knee. Evie nodded. It was our secret signal we used in tricky situations to alert each other to the fact that we needed to get ready to run!

Spinkman made his way, cautiously, to the end of the hedge. A couple more steps around the corner and we'd be exposed!

Evie and I were just about to make a run for it when…

'Oh, Mr Spinkman?' Mrs Wayland called, pulling her phone from her pocket. 'I… I think it may have been my phone that you heard,' she said, holding it up. 'I just received a few messages. Now, shouldn't we… get this over and done with?'

He looked around once more before straightening his tie and walking back to his car.

Phew! That was close!

'He looks nervous,' I whispered to Evie, lining up the frame with my video.

'Yes. Something is definitely going down!'

Spinkman took a step closer to Mrs Wayland. 'Do

you have the money?' he asked.

She pulled an envelope from her purse and handed it to him. 'It's all there,' she said. 'I'm sorry that it had to come to this but—'

'But your son is one uncoordinated surfer,' he said, shaking his head.

'That may be,' she said. 'But if he's going to be accepted into the Goldacre Grammar School for Exceptional Boys, the most *prestigious* grammar school in the country, he needs to notch up as many accolades as I can possibly pay for!'

'I see,' Spinkman said.

'Just as we agreed. Half now,' Mrs Wayland continued, 'and the other half once you announce Daniel as the winner on Saturday.'

We watched as Spinkman smiled and nodded.

'What's she doing?' Evie asked. 'What's in the envelope?'

'Money,' I told her, shaking my head. 'She *paid* Spinkman to announce Daniel as the winner!'

Evie and I looked at each other before saying in unison: 'Bribery!'

CHAPTER SIX

SURF PRESIDENT STANDS DOWN AFTER BRIBERY CLAIMS

NEW PRESIDENT ALLOWS STEIN TO COMPETE IN SURF COMP FINAL!

By Scoop McLaren

The Legion of Preposterously Professional Surfers is in chaos with the sacking of National President, Hal Spinkman, who, as it turns out, is not very professional at all amid claims he accepted a bribe, altering the outcome of the semi-final in the Monster Wave Supreme Grommet Title.

Spinkman was fired after footage of him taking money from a competitor's parent was obtained by *Click!*.

Mrs Doris Wayland offered Spinkman the bribe in

return for her son being named as a finalist and then the subsequent winner of the Monster Wave Supreme Grommet Title.

Click! learned that Mrs Wayland hoped winning the prestigious tournament would help secure her son a place at the exclusive Goldacre Grammar School for Boys.

Speaking exclusively to *Click!* after the shocking incident was exposed, former Vice President and now National President, Leo Levine, said he was pleased to see the back of Spinkman.

'I've never trusted that man, never!' he said. 'His peculiar, pointy nose, his beady eyes and that ghastly colour he turns when he gets all nervous. And now bribery! That sort of tomfoolery is not welcome in our Legion and will not be tolerated.

'I say, good riddance!'

The scandal has led to the reinstatement of competition favourite, Fletcher Stein, who was ousted out of the semi-final in a judgement that left fans and spectators bewildered.

'I am stoked! Absolutely, positively stoked to be back in the competition,' a beaming Stein told *Click!*.

'I've had a few setbacks, that's for sure, but this is turning into the best summer ever!'

Hundreds of keen surfing fans are expected to flock to Five-Mile Beach on Saturday for the final.

With blue, cloudless skies predicted, the competition climax promises to be an event not to be missed after a week of unfortunate bad sportsmanship and outright mayhem.

As always, *Click!* will be front and centre on the sand to bring our readers all the action.

May the best surfer win!

♥

The next morning, Evie and I met Fletcher at the surf café, just after he had finished his final training session with my dad.

Fletcher was super happy to now be back in the competition and Evie and I were super happy that we had solved the case to make it happen.

In even more exciting news, Fletcher's parents, my Aunt Felicity and Uncle Clive, are flying in to watch him compete in the final. Fletcher doesn't know as it's a surprise and I can't wait to see the look on his face when they arrive.

This is turning into the best summer ever indeed!

'So, it was Hal Spinkman who messed with my

phone?' Fletcher asked as we sat lined up along the counter.

'Precisely,' Evie replied. 'He admitted it all to my dad. Mrs Wayland offered him a huge sum to keep you out of the competition somehow.'

'And when tampering with your phone didn't work, they schemed to announce Daniel as the semi-final winner over you,' I added.

'And he would've gone on to win the whole competition too if it wasn't for Scoop's sharp detective skills,' Evie said.

'So much for Deadeye Dan Durnam's Dastardly Curse,' I quipped.

'So much for *what*?' Fletcher asked.

Evie shook her head. 'Never mind,' she said.

'I've really got to hand it to you two again,' Fletcher grinned. 'I know I wouldn't be in the final if it wasn't for you and your spot-on sleuthing.' Then he raised his milkshake. 'Here's to sleuthing!'

Evie giggled as the three of us clinked glasses. 'To sleuthing!' we cried.

'Dyehe, Deivee? Ddluohse dewe dtele Drehctelfe dnie dnoe druoe dtercese degaugnale?' I asked my friend.

Evie thought for a moment. 'Rtonr rerusr, Rssobr.

Rnacr rehr rebr rdetsurtr?' she replied.

'What in the world are you two talking about?' Fletcher asked. 'It sounds like… gibberish!'

'It's our…' I looked around before whispering, '… *secret language*.'

He shook his head. 'You girls are so weird,' he huffed.

'It's not weird,' Evie piped up. 'It's clever. We devised it at the beginning of the summer. It could come in extremely handy one day.'

'Yes, and it means that we can talk freely in front of suspects and they'll never know what we are saying.'

'You got that right,' Fletcher said. 'Well, how does it work?'

'We can't tell you, Fletch,' I said.

'Come on, *please*?'

'No way,' Evie added, shaking her head. 'Not in a million years.'

'Sorry,' I told him. 'It's top secret.'

'Or rpotr rtercesr,' Evie said.

'Huh?' Fletcher asked.

Evie and I looked at each other and burst out laughing, much to Fletcher's annoyance.

What we couldn't tell him is that we take a word and then flip it backwards. Then I add a 'D' to the front of the word and an 'E' to the back. DE – detective editor! Then, after Evie flips her word around, she adds an 'R' to the front and an 'R' to the end. RR – roving reporter!

It took some getting used to, but what new language doesn't?

'You girls are just being silly,' Fletcher said, spinning his chair away from us.

'Rhor, ryllaerr?' Evie said, and we both giggled. 'Rehr rsyasr rewr rerar ryllisr, rpoocsr!'

'Die dknihte dehe dsie dehte dyllise denoe,' I replied.

'Oh, cut it out!' Fletcher protested.

Evie giggled so hard she blew bubbles in her milkshake!

When Mr Mack appeared from the storeroom, whistling and finishing off the last of a chocolate bar, she sat up straight and wiped her mouth.

'Sorry, Mr Mack,' she said. 'I know you don't like any tomfoolery at the counter. Or anywhere within a five-mile radius of the surf café.'

'Well, maybe for just one day every week, we could have some tomfoolery in here,' he smiled. Then he took three oranges from a bowl on the counter and started expertly juggling them. 'Might… brighten the place up a bit,' he said with a smile.

'Wow,' Evie uttered, her brow furrowing. 'You're being *way* weird lately.'

I shot her a look.

'Sorry,' she shuddered. 'Did I say that outside of my head?'

To our complete surprise, Mr Mack just laughed. Then he rolled an orange each towards us. 'I've been thinking,' he said. 'What would you kids say if I made some changes, like... bring in free wi-fi?'

'That'd be awesome!' Fletcher said.

'Yeah,' Evie agreed. 'And you'd get *loads* more customers with free wi-fi.'

He leaned over the counter and smiled. 'That's exactly what I was thinking. Free wi-fi it is!' he sang.

He was acting awfully strange. Nice. Friendly even. Although I must admit Mr Mack is more pleasant to be around these past few days, my detective mind can't shake the feeling that there might be something fishy going on.

As Fletcher and Evie tried to talk Mr Mack into free milkshakes to go along with the free wi-fi, I checked my watch. It was almost time to get Fletcher home for his surprise!

♥

We were no sooner home from the surf café and sprawled around the lounge, watching TV, when Dad drove into the drive. He honked the car horn.

'I wonder what Dad could want,' I said to Fletcher and Evie.

'Probably wants some help with the groceries,' Fletcher replied in an unenthusiastic tone. He dragged himself off the sofa and headed for the door.

'Probably,' Evie said. She winked at me as we made our way outside.

'Mum! Dad!' Fletcher cried as Aunt Felicity and Uncle Clive climbed out of Dad's car. He ran into their arms and they squeezed him tightly.

'Oh, our boy!' Aunt Felicity beamed. 'We've missed you so much!'

'How was Antarctica?' he asked.

'Cold,' Uncle Clive replied, roughing Fletcher's hair. 'It's good to see you, son.'

♥

That night, Dad cooked his famous lasagne for dinner while Evie and I whipped up my speciality –

homemade garlic bread. Dad loves cooking for guests, and I just know Fletcher and his parents will love our homemade dishes.

'Dnace duoye desaelpe dssape dehte dtlase, Deivee?' I asked my roving reporter as we worked on the garlic bread.

'Rylniatrecr,' she replied, handing me the salt shaker.

'Dode douye desilaere dtahte dewe ddevlose dtahte desace dnie ddrocere demite?'

'Rseyr, rosr rewr rdidr!' she beamed. 'Ryayr rsur!'

'Um, exactly what were you two on about in there?' Uncle Clive asked as we brought the bread out to the dining room table and sat down. 'Are you learning another language?'

'Oh, don't bother asking,' Fletcher piped up as he took a seat next to his dad. 'They're all *sworn to secrecy*,' he cooed, as Evie and I giggled.

'We can't go about giving away secrets, Fletcher,' said Evie. 'That's why Scoop is the best detective editor in town!'

'Try the *only* detective editor in town,' he replied.

'And Evie's the best roving reporter,' I said. I turned to my friend and we slapped hands. 'Some things have to remain between the two of us.'

Fletcher just shook his head as he made a beeline

for the lasagne and the garlic bread.

'Never a dull moment around here, folks,' Dad said, shrugging.

'I can see that,' Aunt Felicity laughed. 'Scoop, I can't believe how much you've grown since we saw you last summer,' she said.

I smiled and sat up straight. 'I'm one full inch taller,' I proudly told her.

'I haven't grown at all, Mrs Stein,' Evie lamented as she moved pieces of lasagne around her plate. Then she smiled. 'But Mum says I'm due for a growth spurt any minute now.'

'I'm sure you are, sweetheart,' she laughed.

Aunt Felicity was super kind. She was tall and willowy and had long, wavy blonde hair. She always smelled sweet too, like candied apples.

Uncle Clive was a burly, big fellow, who used to be in the Army, but on the inside, he was all gooey and nice, just like Aunt Felicity.

'So, Fletcher? Are you ready for the final tomorrow?' Dad asked.

'You bet, Uncle Ted,' Fletcher said. 'Thanks to you, I'm all set! And Mr Mack. I haven't forgotten what he taught me.'

'Who is this Mr Mack character?' Uncle Clive asked.

'Well,' Dad started out. 'He—'

'He's a bit of an odd bod really,' Evie chimed in, in between mouthfuls of garlic bread. 'And angry, he's almost always angry.' She frowned. 'Except for lately. Now he's all nice and offering free wi-fi, so... I don't know.'

Confused, Uncle Clive looked over at Dad for an adult explanation.

'He always has been a bit... uptight,' Dad offered, 'but he's a good man and he's been a great help to Fletcher.'

'Well, with everything that's been going on, we must admit, we were almost relieved when you *didn't* make the final, Fletch,' Uncle Clive said. 'A near miss with a motorcycle, bribery... it's all a bit too much, even for a seasoned soldier like me!'

'Don't worry, Dad, all that's over now, thanks to Scoop and Evie,' Fletcher smiled. 'And now that you guys are here to cheer me on, there isn't anything going to stop me from winning the final tomorrow.'

♥

After Evie had gone home and the rest of us had said our goodnights, I snuggled in under the covers and started to think about tomorrow's final. I had to be on my game. It was the biggest thing to hit Higgity Harbour since the Sonny Fink saga, and I wanted my loyal readers to get the very best, up-to-date coverage!

As I drifted off, my thoughts also turned to Mr Mack and his strange behaviour of late. I didn't see the stern man with the fancy suit today. Perhaps whatever problem he seemed to have with Mr Mack was all cleared up? Maybe that was the reason for his good mood and sudden generosity?

In any case, I needed to concentrate on the surf final. Whatever was going on with Mr Mack would have to wait.

♥

HUNDREDS HIT THE SAND FOR SURF FINAL

By Evie Andrews

Sports fans are lining Five-Mile Beach today to watch Higgity Harbour surfing history in the making as young top guns Fletcher Stein and Wallace Arnold battle it out for the prestigious title of Monster Wave Supreme Grommet.

In the lead-up to the event, *Click!* took to the streets to see just who local residents think will walk, or rather surf, away with the title.

'My money is on Fletcher Stein,' said Higgity Harbour Mayor, Tom Willis. 'The boy's been through one heck of a week and is still standing. You can't teach that kind of determination. Fletcher is number one!'

Local golf pro, Noah Proctor, agreed. 'I don't know all that much about surfing, golfing is my thing, but I do know a champion when I see one,' he said. 'Fletcher makes it look easy – a sure sign of a victor ludorum!'

Higgity Harbour's florist extraordinaire, Dempsey Duewater, said she's certain Wallace Arnold will win. 'I think Fletcher has just been lucky thus far,' she said. 'And today, I think that luck is about to run out. Go Wallace!'

In a *Click!* exclusive, Stein said he felt confident going into today's final.

'I know I can win this,' he said, charged with enthusiasm.

'I've been training super hard and I'm as ready as I'll ever be to get out there and catch some waves!'

When approached by *Click!* following his final

training session this morning, Arnold was equally as confident.

'That trophy is as good as mine,' he said.

'Unlike some, I don't need to stoop to terrible tactics to beat Fletcher – I'll win that prize money, fair and square.'

For all the live action of the surf competition final, stick close to your phones and devices, as *Click!* brings you up-to-the-minute coverage of the biggest sports event to hit Higgity Harbour this year!

♥

Despite fine weather and sunny skies predicted, it was a still morning with dark grey clouds rolling in, blanketing the sky over Five-Mile Beach.

The gloomy weather, however, didn't stop a throng of spectators from making their way down to the sand to take in the much-anticipated final.

Evie and I headed to the Surf Life Saving Club. They were giving away free bottles of water to spectators and we wanted to grab some in readiness for a big day ahead. Being a detective editor can be rigorous, hard work sometimes, especially when you're running up and down a beach interviewing people, and it's really very important to stay well hydrated! Dad taught me that.

As we trudged up the sand, I could hear the distant rumblings of thunder.

'Sounds like a storm is brewing,' I told Evie as I checked out the sky.

'It wasn't forecast,' she replied. 'You know, tonight's the night of the full moon during the summer solstice. It could be the curse?'

'Oh, Evie,' I chimed as I strapped on my backpack, but somehow this was making me feel a little unsure myself.

Loaded up with water and everything else I needed for the day – camera, notebook, sparkly silver pen and voice recorder – we met up with Kenny on the sand.

'I suppose you're going to steal the exclusive away from me today, Scoop?' he asked, checking the settings on his camera. 'Because *everybody* wants to get in *Click!*.'

'Don't be daft,' I told him. 'My dad told me that ever since you've taken on being his sports journo, subscriptions to the *Gazette* have almost doubled.'

He looked up and smiled. 'Really?'

'Yes. Believe me, the reading public know what they like, Kenny Dixon, and they really like you.'

Kenny blushed.

The three of us stood at the starting line and watched as surfing fans set up for their best viewing positions on the sand. Children had paddle boards, throwing them onto the sand and jumping atop, trying to imitate Fletcher catching a wave.

Just then, a booming voice rang out over the PA system. 'Ladies and gentlemen, boys and girls, welcome to the Monster Wave Supreme Grommet grand final!' the marshal said, and everyone cheered. 'Would competitors please make their way to the starting line.'

'I'm going over there,' Kenny said, 'to get a good shot of the starting line-up.'

'Okay.'

I looked around and spotted Fletcher and Dad jogging towards us. Following close behind were Aunt Felicity and Uncle Clive.

'All ready, girls?' Dad asked.

'Yep, Mr McLaren,' Evie said. 'I'll get photos of the action and Scoop's all set to interview Fletch, as soon as he wins.'

Fletcher, bouncing up and down nervously, smiled. '*If* I win,' he said. 'But thanks for the vote of confidence, Evie.'

'You nervous, son?' Uncle Clive asked.

'A… a little.'

'Don't worry, it's good to be nervous,' his dad reassured him. 'It's natural. You get too relaxed and you won't perform at your peak.'

'Relaxed? Huh, no chance of that.'

'You'll do fine.'

Fletcher looked around. 'Where's Mr Mack?' he asked. 'When I spoke to him the other day, he promised me he'd be here to watch me in the final.'

'I'm sure he'll be here,' Dad replied.

Fletcher shrugged and then picked up his board. 'I better go,' he said. Aunt Felicity reached out and grabbed him in a hug. 'My ace surfer,' she said. 'Good luck, sweetheart.'

He smiled. 'Thanks, Mum.' Then he jogged off towards the starting line.

'Just… have fun, Fletch!' Dad called, trying to get some last-second coaching in. 'Shred some waves, son!'

Fletcher turned around, jogging backwards, and gave Dad a thumbs up before joining Wallace Arnold at the starting line.

'Where *is* Mr Mack?' Evie turned to me and asked. 'I thought he'd be here for sure.'

I shrugged as I checked my camera. Dad had given it to me ages ago. It was especially good for taking action shots. 'Who knows? Here's the camera,' I said, handing it to her. 'Come on, let's get closer.'

'Sure thing, boss.'

We raced over to the starting line.

'Okay, competitors, your attention please,' the marshal said. 'All finals are ten minutes in duration.'

I looked around at Aunt Felicity and Uncle Clive who were huddled together excitedly, ready to watch the action. Aunt Felicity gave me a thumbs up and I smiled.

'Competitors ready?' the marshal called.

With one blast of a deafening siren, the long-awaited final had begun! The crowd cheered as we watched the boys make their way out into the surf.

Fletcher paddled until the wall of ocean rose up in front of him. Then he was on his feet, effortlessly gliding across the wave while Wallace Arnold lost his balance and crashed into the surf around him.

'Wow, that kid's good,' I heard the marshal say as Fletcher shredded the long wall.

I turned to my dad. 'What do you think?' I asked.

Dad smiled. 'I think this is *definitely* Fletcher's day,' he beamed.

'I wouldn't be too confident, Mr McLaren,' Kenny said, breezing up beside us. 'Wallace Arnold has a tendency to leave his best surfing until last.'

Dad nodded. 'That's true.'

The siren blared again, signalling the end of the first round. Fletcher jogged in, surfboard under arm, looking pleased with himself. He ran up to us.

'Good job, Fletch,' I said, and we high-fived. 'You were awesome out there!'

'Thanks, Scoop.'

I took out my laptop and had just enough time before the final round to update my readers.

STEIN TAKES LEAD IN MONSTER GROMMET FINAL

By Scoop McLaren

BREAKING: After the first round of the Monster Wave Supreme Grommet final, it appears that Fletcher Stein is slightly ahead of rival, Wallace Arnold, with one all-important final round to go.

Stein had an almost faultless first set; however, in the

game of surfing, the tide can turn pretty quickly!

As dark clouds threaten above and spectators remain glued to the action, just who will claim today's top prize is anyone's guess.

Stick around and see it first in *Click!* – the only paper to bring you real-time updates and exclusive interviews!

CHAPTER SEVEN

Just as I clicked the button to send my update out into cyberspace, the grumbling of thunder rolling in, teamed with the sound of the siren, filled the air.

'Would competitors please line up for the final round,' the marshal called.

'This is it,' Fletcher said, running past us. 'Make sure you get some good shots, Evie.'

Evie held up the camera and smiled. 'Sure thing, champ! Go get 'em!'

As many had predicted, Wallace Arnold made a brave comeback after his disappointing first set and surfed like a demon in the final round!

As graceful as a dancer, he rode the lip of a wave like he was glued to it. The crowd gasped in awe as he pivoted back and forth, moving so fast it seemed as if nothing could bring him down.

My poor dad watched, in between his fingers,

as Fletcher fell, diving headfirst into a wave – *crash, boom, bang!* – until Wallace Arnold was the last one standing.

'Oh no,' Aunt Felicity cried, standing on her tiptoes to get a better view of her son. 'Is Fletcher all right?'

'He's fine,' Uncle Clive replied. 'The only thing he's hurt is his pride.'

With one final blast of the siren, it was over. The boys ran in with their boards and gathered around the scoreboard.

'What do you think, Dad?' I asked.

He shook his head. 'It's going to be awfully close, love,' he said.

Fletcher just had time to come out of his surfing suit when the head marshal's voice echoed in the microphone.

'Okay, everyone,' the marshal said, 'the final results are in.'

Fletcher joined us next to the podium. I looked over at him, his face brimming with excitement. Dad was right – it had been a long week, and, win or lose, I was so proud of my friend.

'Hey, Fletch,' I whispered. He looked over at me and smiled, and I snapped a picture with my phone.

'And now, what you've all been waiting for,' the

marshal said. 'Newly appointed National President, Leo Levine, will announce the winner.'

A hush fell over the crowd as Mr Levine took to the microphone. 'In first place, the winner of the Higgity Harbour Monster Wave Supreme Grommet Title is…'

Just then a frightening crack of thunder rang out, prompting some in the crowd to scream! Then the heavens opened up and rain – hard, pelting rain – fell in bucketloads from the sky.

Mr Levine looked up to the angry sky above us. 'Okay, folks, we better wrap this up quickly! The winner is… Fletcher Stein! Come on up here, Fletcher!'

Fletcher ran up to the podium and collected his trophy and prize money before the crowd began to disperse. People started running in every which direction, shrieking and bumping into each other to get out of the storm.

'Yes, um… congrats, Fletcher, well done,' Mr Levine said as he quickly turned on his heel and ran for cover as well.

It was complete madness! People were scurrying around like hurried ants, and I'd lost sight of Dad, Evie and Fletcher.

In amongst all the mayhem, I looked up to the

surf shop to see Mr Mack, standing outside. I waved at him and gave him a thumbs up in celebration of Fletcher's victory.

He waved back before he turned and walked away.

♥

STEIN STORMS HOME IN MONSTER WAVE FINAL

By Scoop McLaren

In one of the most controversial competitions in modern surfing history, Fletcher Stein has won the Higgity Harbour Monster Wave Supreme Grommet Title!

Stein out-surfed competitor Wallace Arnold at Five-Mile Beach today, winning the glittering first place trophy along with an impressive £3,000 in prize money.

Surfing and competing in competitions since the age of five, Stein said winning the local competition was indeed something special.

'I come to Higgity Harbour every summer – it's like my second home – so to win here is awesome!' he told *Click!*.

Stein thanked his coaches, Ted McLaren and Juniper

Mack, for helping him train.

'The trophy is as much theirs as it is mine,' he said.

Throughout the competition, Stein dodged numerous sabotage attempts by rival surfing parents; however, he rose above all obstacles to take out the title.

As celebrations were cut short by an unpredicted storm, a party is being held in Stein's honour at the Higgity Harbour Surf Life Saving Club today, commencing at 2 p.m., and an open invitation is extended to all in the community to attend.

Well surfed, Fletcher, well surfed!

♥

As soon as the latest issue of *Click!* hit cyberspace, Evie and I rushed out of the door to join the party that was being thrown in celebration of Fletcher's incredible win.

We ran all the way from my house in the storm to get there, and when we arrived, the surf club was alive with celebration.

Kenny and my dad were there, handing out food and making sure everybody had a drink. Aunt Felicity and Uncle Clive were there too, beaming from ear to ear after Fletcher's victory.

We had been at the surf club for about fifteen minutes and were demolishing some refreshing colas when Dad sailed up to us. He was wearing an apron, proudly in charge of preparing and handing out sausage sandwiches with homemade tomato relish.

'Hey, girls, did you get the paper out?' he asked.

'Sure did, Mr McLaren,' Evie cooed. 'It's swimming around cyberspace as we speak.'

'And Evie took an awesome picture of Fletcher riding the waves to go with it, Dad,' I added. 'Best front page yet!'

Dad smiled. 'Well, I can't wait to read it.'

I looked around. 'Where's Fletcher?'

'Fletcher went up to the surf shop café to thank Mr Mack for helping to train him and to invite him to the celebration,' Dad said. Then he looked at his watch. 'But that was twenty minutes ago.'

When another ten minutes had passed, and Fletcher had still not appeared, I began to feel uneasy.

'Something feels off,' I told Evie. 'Fletcher would *not* want to be missing his own party.'

'Do you want me to run over to the surf café and check?' Evie asked.

'Would you?'

She sat her cola down. 'Sure thing, DE,' she replied.

'Thanks, RR.'

After another ten minutes had passed, with no sign of anybody, I sent Evie a message. When she didn't answer, I decided to go and check for myself. Dad, Fletcher's parents and Kenny came with me, leaving Mayor Tom Willis in charge of the party until we returned.

It had stopped raining and we got to the surf shop café to find it closed, with not a person in sight.

'Where are they?' Dad asked while looking through the windows. 'I distinctly heard Fletcher say he was coming here.'

'Evie was meant to be here too! Let's check out the car park,' I said.

We rushed around the corner of the surf shop café and into the deserted car park.

'I just *know* something isn't right,' I said, searching around for clues. It wasn't long before I found one. 'Ah-huh! If Mr Mack, Evie and Fletcher were here, they sure left in a hurry.'

Dad stepped forward. 'What do you mean, Scoop?' he asked.

I leaned down to see a number of muddy footprints on the ground. 'There was a struggle,' I said, 'right here, where Mr Mack's car was parked.'

'Wow,' Kenny said. 'What else can you tell us, Scoop?'

I continued my search. I thoroughly examined the ground near the footprints until something unexpected caught my eye. 'Oh no,' I said.

'What is it, love?' Dad asked, scanning the ground near my feet.

'Dad, you better call Sergeant Andrews and fast,' I told him.

Uncle Clive turned to me. 'But why, Scoop? What happened here? Where's Fletcher?'

'And Evie?' Kenny cried.

'They're in trouble,' I replied, looking down at the one word my roving reporter had managed to scribble into the mud before she disappeared.

RPLEHR

♥

NEWLY CROWNED SURF CHAMPION AND ACE REPORTER MISSING!

By Scoop McLaren

Not more than an hour after winning the Higgity Harbour Monster Wave Supreme Grommet Title, teenage surfing sensation, Fletcher Stein, is missing!

Click! uncovered his disappearance after Fletcher failed to show up at a planned celebration thrown in his honour.

Click!'s very own roving reporter, Evie Andrews, is also unaccounted for, along with local surf shop café owner, Juniper Mack, who trained Fletcher for part of the competition.

Fletcher Stein is 13 years old, about 165cm in height and has sandy blond hair and brown eyes. Evie Andrews is 13 years old, around 150cm in height, with black hair and blue eyes. Juniper Mack is 50 years old, about 183cm in height and has long, silvery grey hair.

Images will be uploaded shortly.

Anyone who may have sighted the trio, after the competition came to an abrupt and stormy end, is urged to contact Police Sergeant Mick Andrews at Higgity Harbour Police Station or call Crime Crusaders on 1 700 STOP CRIME.

More coverage of this breaking story as it comes to hand. Watch this space!

♥

As soon as I uploaded the pictures, I was back on the case.

That same afternoon, Dad, Kenny, Fletcher's parents and I met with Sergeant Andrews at the police station, where we filled him in on all we knew.

'There has been foul play here, Sergeant. Fletcher and Evie are in trouble!' I told him.

'But what makes you so sure, love?' Dad asked. 'Perhaps there's a logical explanation for all of this?'

I toyed with the idea of telling Dad, of telling them all, that it was the clever clue that Evie had managed to write in the mud that made me so certain, but then I couldn't without giving our secret language away!

What would Evie want you to do, Scoop?

I knew exactly what my reporter buddy would say.

'I… I'm sorry, Dad,' I stammered. 'I can't tell you *how* I know for certain. You'll need to trust me on this. I know they're in trouble, I just know they are.'

Dad and Sergeant Andrews looked at each other.

'You really think Evie is in danger, Scoop?' Sergeant Andrews frowned.

I nodded.

'I've rarely known Scoop to be wrong about something like this, Mick. Wouldn't hurt to check it out, would it?' Dad asked.

Sergeant Andrews shook his head. 'No, and if my Evie's in trouble...' he said. He spun around and picked up his phone. 'I'll issue a BOLO to all officers from here to Cascade Point, pronto.'

'BOLO?' Kenny asked.

'Be On the Look Out.'

'You better put one out for Juniper Mack too,' Dad said.

'Yes,' I agreed.

'Will do,' Sergeant Andrews said.

'In any case, Fletcher has his phone,' Dad said. 'I'm sure he'll manage to tell us what's going on.'

'No, he doesn't,' Uncle Clive said, pulling Fletcher's phone from his pocket. 'He gave it to me to hold before the final and I never got the chance to give it back.'

'Oh, dear,' I said.

'Scoop?' Dad asked. 'Do you think... do you think Juniper Mack has anything to do with Fletcher and

Evie's disappearance? I mean… he may have been the last person to see them. And now he's nowhere to be found either.'

I sighed. 'I'm not sure, Dad,' I told him. 'Perhaps someone who was on the beach at the final today is after Fletcher for his prize money? It was awarded in cash.'

'Hmm… perhaps,' Dad said.

'Maybe Mr Mack and Evie intervened and now… they're missing too? Perhaps—'

'Perhaps Mr Mack *is* the culprit?' Kenny chimed in. 'He has been acting really strangely lately, you've seen it yourself, Scoop!'

'At this stage, we can't discount any theory,' I said, checking my phone. I thought Evie might have managed to message me, but no such luck.

'You need to find them, Scoop,' Uncle Clive cried, stepping forward and taking my hand. 'You need to find them and bring them home.'

I looked over at Aunt Felicity. She was gazing out of the office window and had tears streaming down her face. Then I turned to see Sergeant Andrews. He was pacing back and forth, barking out orders to his constables over the phone. Although he was trying to hide it well, I just knew he was worried too.

I'd always had Evie to lean on, in times like this, but not now. My best friend was missing! I felt like crying too, like running into Dad's arms and bursting into tears. I wasn't even sure I could do this without Evie beside me. But I had to try. I knew she'd be counting on me!

I whipped out my phone. 'Sergeant Andrews, can you do me a favour?'

'Of course.'

'I'm going to send you a picture I took a few days ago, a licence plate number. Can you track down who the owner is?'

'Yes, no problem.'

I sent him the picture I'd managed to snap of the angry man's car outside Mr Mack's surf café. I had a suspicion that he could somehow be involved in all of this.

'Got it!' Sergeant Andrews said.

'Awesome.'

I took a deep breath, picked up my backpack and headed for the door.

'If anyone needs me, I'll be hitting the streets right now.'

'What for?' Kenny asked.

'To investigate, Kenny,' I said. 'To investigate!'

'Hold on, Scoop,' Dad called, standing between me and the door. 'You be careful, young lady. There's quite possibly three people now missing in Higgity Harbour. I don't want you to be the fourth.'

'I'll go with her, Mr M,' Kenny offered, springing to his feet. 'She'll be safe with me. That okay, Scoop?'

'Yes, fine, just… let's go!'

CHAPTER EIGHT

Mrs Bailey was the first resident we came across when we took to the streets of Higgity Harbour, asking questions and searching for clues.

She was leaving Betty Wiseman's hairdressing salon, primping her new hairdo in shop windows as she passed by.

'Hey, Mrs Bailey!' I called as we chased after her. She stopped and gave us a wave.

'Your hair looks sick!' I said once I'd caught up to her. '*Really* sick!'

Mrs Bailey's face fell. 'Sick? Oh no! That's definitely *not* the look I was going for.'

'Don't worry,' I said. 'By "sick", I actually mean great. Your hair looks great.'

'You really think so?' she asked, checking herself out in the hardware store window behind us.

'I really think so. Now, we're wondering if you can

help us?' I showed her the picture of Fletcher I had taken on my phone earlier at the beach. 'Have you seen this boy? Or my best friend, Evie Andrews?'

She took my phone and studied the picture. 'Why, yes. I saw the boy not too long ago. In the salon, while I was getting my hair done,' she said. 'But I haven't seen Evie today.'

'In the salon?' Kenny frowned. 'Fletcher was in the salon?'

'Hmm…' she thought for a moment. 'No… I mean… yes, I did see him, but it was on the front page of *Click!*. All the girls were reading it from one of those… tablet thingies and showing it around the salon. It was a fabulous photo. Did you take it, Scoop?'

I sighed. 'No, Evie did. Mrs Bailey, have you seen Fletcher *in the flesh*, this afternoon at any time?'

'Oh, no, dear. I wouldn't know the boy if I did see him. I'm not really into surfing,' she said, squinting up her nose. 'I don't mind taking a dip in the local public swimming pool every now and then, if it's *excruciatingly* hot, but—'

'Mrs Bailey, if I send this photo to your phone, can you please keep an eye out for him?' I asked.

'Of course but you can *send* a photo to my

phone?' she asked curiously.

'Yes. What's your mobile number?'

'Oh, I don't have a mobile phone. Silly things. If somebody wants to reach me badly enough, they'll find me. I can give you my number at home? Can you send the photo through to my phone on the kitchen wall?'

'Um… no,' I said. 'Never mind. Have a nice day!'

We trudged off, leaving Mrs Bailey continuing to check her reflection as she ventured off down the street.

Outside the butcher's shop, Sid Corman offered up an interesting explanation.

'Aliens,' he said, sitting on a bench while waiting for a taxi to take him home.

'Sorry?' I asked.

'Think about it, Scoop! No *human* has surfing talent like that. The boy is an alien and he's been called home to the mother ship. How else do you explain his spooky disappearance? And that thunderstorm? It simply came out of nowhere! It's all the work of…' he looked around before whispering, '…extraterrestrials, I tell you.'

Kenny rolled his eyes and was just about to open his mouth. 'Thanks, Mr Corman,' I said, wheeling around in the other direction. 'We'll certainly keep that in mind!'

Next, we hit the town square where we found Imogen Blaxland, sitting under an elm tree, sucking on a lemon-flavoured ice block and reading an article on her laptop.

'Hi, Imogen,' I said, plonking down next to her.

'Oh, hi, Scoop,' she replied. 'Kenny Dixon.'

'Hey, Imogen.'

'I thought you were refusing to call me Scoop?' I asked her.

'What's today?'

'Saturday,' I replied.

'I shall call you Scoop on Saturdays and… Tuesdays.'

'You are *so* peculiar,' Kenny said, shaking his head and folding his arms. 'What are you reading?'

'If you must know, nosy boots, I'm reading a very interesting article that claims that eighty-one per cent of all the people in this country *may* have some link to royal blood. Those odds are simply fantastic!'

'Are you *still* trying to prove you're a royal?' I asked.

She held her laptop up. 'It says right here that if you have suspicions about your ancestors, you should definitely follow them up because it isn't unheard of for…' she gulped, like she couldn't bring herself to say it, '…*commoners*, to have links to royal blood.'

'Okay, good luck with that, but have you seen Fletcher anywhere? Or Evie,' I asked. 'And please don't give us the runaround because this is really important, Imogen.'

'Almost as important as you trying to fit into the royal family,' Kenny quipped.

She gave Kenny a death stare before turning back to me. 'Sorry. I read about how they were missing in *Click!*. But I haven't seen them. If I *were* royalty, Scoop, I'd order all the Queen's horses and all the Queen's men out to look for them, but, alas…' She sighed.

'Well, if you happen to become royalty in the next hour or so, can you let us know?' I said, running off. 'Come on, Kenny, let's go.'

'Bye, Imogen,' he called.

'Ta-ta,' she replied.

'Let's head back to Main Street,' I said. 'There's no one else around here.'

We spotted Jeremiah Turntable, owner of the local supermarket, standing on the pavement outside his store, watering planter boxes. We carefully crossed Main Street and ran over to him.

'Mr Turntable!' I called. 'Do you have a minute?'

'Oh, hiya, Scoop, Kenny,' he said. 'What are you

two up to?'

'Have you heard the news?' I asked.

'What news?'

'I know you're awfully busy, probably too busy to read *Click!*, but Fletcher Stein, the boy who just won the surfing competition, and my best friend Evie are missing.'

'Possibly Juniper Mack too,' Kenny added.

'Juniper Mack, you say?'

'Yes.'

'Well, I did see him. About thirty minutes ago!' he cried. 'I thought it was strange, he was driving like a mad lunatic! I even called out for him to slow down, but he just took off, like a rocket!'

A lead!

'Which direction did he go in?' I asked.

♥

Back at the police station, Kenny and I burst through the door into Sergeant Andrews' office.

'I have a lead!' I cried.

'Did you find Fletcher?' Aunt Felicity said. 'Is he all right?'

'And Evie?' Sergeant Andrews added. 'Where is she?'

'Do you know where Mr Mack is, Scoop?' Dad asked. 'Is he missing too?'

'Okay, everyone,' Kenny said, jumping up. 'Just give Scoop some space, please.'

Thanks, Kenny!

A million different thoughts were whirling around in my head. I needed to get them straight.

I swallowed down hard and took a deep breath.

'We just spoke to Jeremiah Turntable and he said he saw Mr Mack driving *furiously* down Main Street, not more than thirty minutes ago,' I told them.

Sergeant Andrews turned to me. 'Was Evie in the car?' he said.

'What about Fletcher?' Uncle Clive asked.

I shook my head. 'No, I'm afraid it was just Mr Mack. We need to find that car and we need to act fast. From the manner in which Mr Turntable described Mr Mack's driving, it seems to me that he was trying to get away from the harbour and fast. I now feel Fletcher and Evie are in grave danger! Dad, can you drive us?'

'Of course,' he said, grabbing his car keys from his pocket.

'I'll get every available car out there too!' Sergeant Andrews cried. 'Clive? Felicity? Would you mind going back to the surf café and staying put? Just in case they return?'

'Of course,' Aunt Felicity said, grabbing her handbag.

'We'll go there right now,' Uncle Clive replied.

'Okay, everyone,' I said, making a run for the door. 'We better hurry, I have a funny feeling!'

♥

Sergeant Andrews had run the licence plate number and had found that the car belonged to a Mr Simon Pratt, manager of a bank in Cascade Point. He dug a little further and after speaking to Mr Pratt, he also learned that Mr Mack's café was in trouble, *big* trouble.

'According to Sergeant Andrews, Mr Mack owes the bank a lot of money and the café is barely turning a profit,' I told Dad and Kenny as we made our way around Higgity Harbour with Kenny in the front seat and me in the back.

'Ah-huh! That would explain why he took Fletcher,' Kenny said.

'Indeed!' I replied. 'Fletcher just won three thousand pounds in cold, hard cash! And Mr Mack is penniless! My guess is that he's stolen the money and has now made a run for it, away from here. Away from his failing business and—'

'Away from the one person he knows has the capability of working this all out,' Kenny said. Then he turned to me and smiled. 'You, Scoop!'

'But why take Evie too, love?' Dad asked. 'He'd have no use for her.'

'I bet my friend witnessed what had happened to Fletcher,' I said, choking back tears. 'And knowing Evie, she wouldn't be about to just stand by and watch it happen. She's a fighter,' I smiled, swallowing the lump in my throat. 'Especially for her friends. I'm almost certain that if we find Mr Mack, Fletcher and Evie won't be far away.'

'I can't believe Juniper Mack would do such a thing,' Dad said, turning into Maple Drive. 'He's always struck me as a decent fellow. He even saved you and Evie from Ace Broadmeyer, Scoop.'

'I know, Dad, but all the evidence points to him. He's desperately in need of money, Fletcher just won three thousand pounds and is now missing, and we have an eyewitness that says he saw Mr Mack driving like a crazy person, most probably to get away. If I come up with a stronger suspect, I'll let you know, but for now, our mission is to find Juniper Mack.' As I uttered these words, more thoughts started bouncing in my head. Could I truly believe that Mr Mack was a money thief? He was a grumpy man, he might have had some financial issues with the café, but something didn't add up. I was lost in my trail of ideas when Dad slowed down.

'Okay. Any idea where we should head, Scoop?' Dad asked. 'I feel like I'm just driving around in circles.'

'My only suggestion is that we cover every avenue out of here. He'll be wanting to get away, and fast.'

'Okay, love.'

'Please keep your eyes peeled, guys. I need to inform my readers on our current progress.'

I pulled my laptop out from underneath the back seat and quickly began typing.

♥

SUPER SLEUTH ON THE TRAIL OF THIEF

By Scoop McLaren

BREAKING: Loyal readers, this breaking news comes

to you from out in the field as I, detective editor Scoop McLaren, chase down a suspect that I believe may be behind the mysterious disappearance of surfer champion, Fletcher Stein, and *Click!*'s own roving reporter, Evie Andrews, today.

I am currently on the road, searching for the alleged culprit who I suspect took Fletcher, against his will, for the £3,000 prize money he won in today's final.

As time is of the essence, dear readers, I must sign off, but be sure to stay tuned, as updates will be posted as events unfold!

♥

I could hear the whir of police sirens in the distance and although this mystery was nowhere near solved, the sound of a mighty police presence in our little harbour was reassuring.

'Anyone see anything?' Dad asked as we continued driving around every street in the harbour.

'Afraid not, Mr M,' Kenny said. 'Maybe Mr Turntable was mistaken after all?'

Suddenly my phone dinged. *Perhaps a message from Evie!*

I checked the screen.

'Oh, wow,' I said out loud. 'She's done it!'

'What is it, Scoop?' Kenny asked.

'It's an app Evie and I use, a special sleuthing app where we can pinpoint each other's location. She's managed to let me know exactly where she is!' I cried.

'Excellent, Scoop!' Dad smiled. 'Where is she?'

I pressed a few buttons and waited for the location to be revealed.

She's all right! I told myself. *And not only is my best friend okay, she's helping me solve this mystery!*

'Got a location yet, Scoop?' Kenny asked.

'Just a couple more seconds… bingo! Dad, head for… High Cliff Road!'

'High Cliff Road?' he asked. 'There's nothing down that road except the sawmill and an old beach house that nobody's lived in for years.'

'The beach house, Dad. That's where she is!'

But as my dad turned the corner and headed to the other side of town, a thought crossed my mind. I'd been in this situation before, with Sonny Fink. Sonny tricked us into going to the old abandoned warehouse on the wharf, only to lock us inside!

'Hold on, Dad, wait!' I told him. 'Please, pull over.'

Dad turned the car off the road and shut down the engine. He turned around in his seat. 'What's wrong, love?' he asked.

'Yeah, Scoop, what's going on?' Kenny frowned.

'Maybe… maybe it's a trap?'

Dad and Kenny looked at each other.

'Perhaps it's just a ploy to take us to the *wrong* location, while Mr Mack makes his getaway?'

'You think someone else sent the location? To trick you?' Kenny asked.

I sighed. I could feel my head whirling. *Think, Scoop, think!*

'It's your call, Scoop,' Dad said.

We were running out of time. *What to do? WHAT TO DO?*

I put Sonny Fink out of my mind. That case was well and truly solved. I decided to take a chance!

'Head to the old beach house, Dad,' I told him, and he fired up the engine again.

'Okay, love.'

As he pulled back onto the road, Kenny turned to face me. 'You sure about this, Scoop? You sure we're not walking into a big trap?'

I stared out of the window. The sun was going down and darkness was creeping in.

'Time will tell, Kenny,' I told him. 'Time will tell.'

CHAPTER NINE

As we passed the sawmill on High Cliff Road, I watched as workers were hurriedly loading logs onto the very last truck of the day, trying to beat the fast-approaching darkness.

Once they were out of sight, I knew we were alone... sailing further and further away from the safety of our little town.

Night was settling in as we made our way up the windy road to the cliff top, the headlights and the full moon now our only guide.

When we reached the top, Dad turned into 274 High Cliff Road – the old beach house. As we neared the house, Dad switched the car lights off, just to be on the safe side. In the moonlight I could see the windows of the beach house, boarded up with careless imprecision. It painted a picture of neglect and desolation, sitting high above the ocean on a cliff top.

Even over the whir of the car's engine, I could hear the sound of waves crashing below.

'Look!' Kenny cried as Dad pulled into the weed-ridden circular driveway. 'At the side – it's Mr Mack's car!'

'Okay, cool heads, everyone,' Dad said.

'I'll call Sergeant Andrews,' Kenny said as we all piled out of Dad's car. 'He'll have his officers here in no time.'

'Good idea, son,' Dad replied.

'No time's not good enough, I'm afraid,' I said as I trudged towards the abandoned vehicle. 'I have to find my friends!'

'Scoop, wait!' Dad cried, putting his hand out to stop me. 'This is too dangerous. We'll just wait here for the police to arrive.'

'But, Dad…'

Then Kenny passed my dad his phone.

'Sergeant Andrews wants to talk to you, Mr M,' he said. 'And he doesn't sound happy.'

Dad took the phone. 'Yes… yes… oh no… all right. Thanks, Mick.' He hung up.

'What's going on, Dad?' I asked.

'I've got bad news, I'm afraid,' he said. 'The police can't get here, not for a while anyway. A fully loaded log truck has just overturned on High Cliff Bridge. They can't get past, so they're on foot.'

'On foot!' I cried. 'That could take half an hour or more!'

'I know, love,' Dad said. 'But what else can we do?'

'There doesn't seem to be anyone around,' Kenny said. 'Let's check out the car and we might find a clue.'

Great thinking, Kenny!

Dad walked over to the car and put his hand on the bonnet. 'Still warm,' he said. 'Hasn't been here for long.'

Then I heard an odd sound.

'Everybody, hush!' I said. 'I can hear something.'

The air was still but suddenly everyone heard a faint thumping sound. Then we heard, 'Is anybody out there? *Hellllllp!*'

'It's coming from the car's boot,' I called. I raced towards it.

'Henley Sarah McLaren!' Dad cried as he and Kenny followed. 'Be careful!'

As we got closer, the banging and the cries for help became louder. It was clear to me exactly who the voice inside belonged to – my roving reporter!

'Is somebody out there?' she shouted. 'Get me out of here!'

'It's Evie!' I cried. 'Don't worry, Evie, we're here to rescue you!' I turned to Dad and Kenny. 'But... how do we get her out?'

Kenny looked around. 'Scoop, what's that yellow thing hanging from your backpack?' he asked.

I whirled around and around, like a dog chasing its own tail. 'It's just a pretty zip opener with a heart on the end,' I said, stopping and taking the pack off. 'Evie gave it to me for my birthday.'

'Can I see it?' Kenny asked. I took the long, thin opener off the zip and handed it to him. 'Okay if I destroy it?'

'Well, no, not—'

But it was too late. Kenny had taken the bright yellow sheath off to reveal a piece of thin wire. 'I can use this to fiddle with the lock and get the boot open,' he said.

'We have another sharp detective mind here,' Dad said, patting his sports journo on the back.

As Evie continued to bang loudly, Kenny worked away at the lock. 'Got it!' he said, and the boot lifted.

Evie sat up, coughing and breathing heavily, looking around. She seemed a bit shaken, but the fresh air was obviously helping as her breathing quickly returned to normal.

I grabbed my best friend and gave her the biggest hug I could muster. 'Thank goodness we found you!' I said. 'Nice work using that detective app!'

'So, it worked?' she smiled as Dad and I helped her out of the boot. 'In amongst all the mayhem I must've dropped my phone, but I managed to find an old tablet in the boot of the car!'

'How did you end up in the car boot, Evie?' Dad asked. 'What happened at the surf café this afternoon?'

'And where's Fletcher?' Kenny added.

She gulped down hard. 'First of all, I knew you would find me, Scoop,' she smiled and we high-fived. 'I went to the surf café, to find Fletcher and I found him all right – tied up in the boot of Mr Mack's car! I had no sooner scribbled a message to Scoop in the mud to alert her of the situation, when I looked behind me to see Mr Mack. Then, before I knew it, he had bundled me into the boot as well!'

'Wow, you must've been so scared,' I told her.

'I was,' she said. 'Fletch and I both were. Then after what seemed like hours of driving, we stopped…' she looked around, '… here, and Mr Mack let Fletcher out of the boot.'

'Well, where are they now?' Kenny asked.

We all turned towards the dark and eerie beach house.

♥

The door to the old beach house made an awful whining sound as Dad slowly opened it and we made our way in. It was deathly quiet inside. The only sound now was the crashing of those waves on the rocks below the cliff.

My eyes scanned the darkened room – pieces of furniture were covered in dusty white sheets and they looked like ghosts. Shabby old curtains covered three big windows, the moonlight sneaking in through tears along the top and bottom, illuminating the silvery cobwebs that had taken up residence in every corner.

I felt Evie grab my hand. 'Scary,' she whispered. I nodded and we pushed on.

The floorboards creaked with every step we took and then, suddenly, out of the corner of my eye, I spied movement. I turned.

'What's that?' I cried.

We heard a loud *ding, dong, ding!*

Evie immediately sprang into karate mode. 'Hi-ya!' she screamed, jumping backwards.

Ding, dong, ding!

'Arghhhhh!' I screamed, grabbing hold of Kenny's arm.

It was a creature, of some sort, with yellow eyes peering out at us through the darkness. Whatever it was, it was moving fast!

'It's okay, it's okay,' Dad said, walking towards a corner. 'It was a rat, running across the piano keys,' he told us.

'Oh, jeez, Evie,' Kenny said, holding his chest. 'You scared the life out of me!'

'Sorry,' she shrugged.

'Let's continue on,' Dad said. 'Stay close.'

We filed, one by one, into the next room, the kitchen. There were no curtains in the room, allowing for much more moonlight to guide us. The smell was not pleasant, like something I once smelled on a school excursion to the local waste centre.

'Yuck, poo,' Evie gasped, and I saw her pull her jumper up over her nose.

'Don't worry, it's probably just piles of rubbish,' Kenny offered, but it didn't make us feel any better.

Then a loud noise rang out from behind us... *bang, boom, bang!*

'Arghhhh!' Kenny shouted and we turned to see a

large cupboard door break away from its hinges and land on the dusty floor behind him.

'You okay, son?' Dad asked.

'Yes,' he replied. 'But that was close!'

Moving along, we came to a long hall with six doorways and at the end was a steep staircase that ascended into darkness.

'We should check every room,' Kenny said, shoulders back and steeling himself for the task at hand.

Dad turned to us. 'Okay, kids. Kenny, Evie, you check down here. Scoop and I will head upstairs. If you come across Mr Mack, scream for all you're worth and we'll come running.' Then he checked his watch. 'The police should be here soon.'

'Right, Mr M,' Kenny said, and he and Evie split off from us.

Dad and I searched every room on the first floor but found nothing.

'One more flight, Dad,' I said, nodding towards the top of the stairwell. 'The... the attic.'

We both looked up to the door off the very last staircase in the house.

'The only door left,' Dad said. 'Doesn't sound like Kenny and Evie have found anyone. So, if Juniper and

Fletcher are in this house, they're in that attic.'

'This is it then,' I nodded.

He rested his hand on my shoulder. 'Ready, love?'

'As I'll ever be,' I replied.

We climbed upstairs and when we reached the top I could hear a dull banging noise, coming from the cupboard by the staircase.

Moving quickly, I kicked away an old chair that had been used to keep the cupboard door shut and opened it carefully.

'Fletcher!' I whispered with a big smile and we hugged.

'Fletch! Are you all right?' Dad asked softly.

'Yes, Uncle Ted, I'm okay, but… it's Mr Mack! He took me and Evie,' he stammered, pointing at the attic's door.

Dad nodded. I watched as Dad's shaking hand took hold of the doorknob. 'Be careful, Dad,' I said. 'It sounds as if Mr Mack has lost his mind. Who knows what he's capable of?'

'Scoop and Fletcher, just stay behind me,' Dad said. 'Whatever happens, keep close.'

'We will, Dad.'

One… two… three…

Dad turned the knob and flung the door wide

open. 'Ah-huh!' he cried.

There was a lamp sitting on a table, illuminating the room, and across in the corner we spied Mr Mack. He was strangely standing by the window, staring out at the dark ocean in the moonlight.

Dad turned to Mr Mack and shouted, 'All along, you were planning to kidnap Fletcher and steal his prize money? No wonder you didn't show on the beach this morning.'

Mr Mack. On the beach this morning. Waving. Suddenly it dawned on me. *Oh no!* My brain was buzzing. I was starting to understand what was really happening here. This mystery was going into a completely different direction!

'How could you, Juniper?' Dad continued. 'After all these years, an upstanding resident of Higgity Harbour and now... now this! Turn around. What do you have to say for yourself?'

Nothing had happened because of a silly curse. One single person was behind all of this. I stepped forward. 'Wait one moment, Dad!' I cried. 'This man is *not* Mr Mack!'

CHAPTER TEN

The man finally turned around to face us.

'What do you mean, love?' Dad asked me. 'Of course, it's Mr Mack – look at him!'

'No, Dad,' I said, taking a step closer. 'It's not *Juniper* Mack! Today, on the beach, after everyone had left and the competition was over, I waved to Mr Mack from the shoreline and he waved back.'

'So?'

'So, the *real* Mr Mack is short-sighted. He told us so. The *real* Mr Mack would never have been able to see me. It's all making sense now. The real Mr Mack also detests chocolate. Yet that day at the surf café when *this man* was talking about free wi-fi, he was eating a chocolate bar! And lastly, about the free wi-fi – Mr Mack is a Luddite – he's not one bit interested in technology. I doubt he'd even know what wi-fi is!'

'Nice work, Scoop!' Dad said. 'But… if this man

isn't Mr Mack, who is he?'

'This man is an imposter!' I cried.

'Scoop McLaren, detective editor,' the man smiled. 'I knew I'd never fool you.'

Just then the door to the attic flung wide open and in tumbled Evie and Kenny… with Mr Mack!

'Look who we found, tied up in a cupboard on the second floor!' Kenny cried.

'That man is my twin brother,' Mr Mack said, pointing to the imposter. 'Harding Mack, and he escaped from prison two days ago. He's had me holed up here ever since!'

'That's why he was so nice to us,' Evie quipped. 'Because it wasn't him! Free wi-fi, pfft! I should've known Mr Mack could never be that nice.' Then she turned to him. 'No offence.'

We watched as Mr Mack walked over to his brother.

'Harding?' Mr Mack exclaimed. 'You know you'll never get away with this. You know you'll eventually have to go back to prison.' Then he stared him up and down. 'Why… you're wearing the *exact* same clothes as me!'

'I know why… This man had plans to steal Mr Mack's identity,' I said. Then I turned to him. 'Isn't that right?'

'Shut up, shut up, all of you!' Harding cried.

'The police are on their way. They'll be here at any minute,' I told Harding.

'Give it up, Harding,' Kenny said. 'There's no way out now. It's over.'

'On the contrary, I have you all right where I want you,' he smirked.

'What do you mean?' Evie asked.

'This!' he cried. Then, from out of nowhere, he charged towards Mr Mack, tackling him to the ground.

'What's he doing?' Evie squealed.

'You girls stand back!' Dad warned.

We watched as the pair wrestled and rolled around on the floor. They tumbled, backwards and forwards, and then around and around again. It was making my head spin!

Finally, they parted, and both men jumped to their feet. It was hard to make head nor tail of it, who was who, since they were both wearing the same white T-shirt, blue jeans and black boots.

'Hang on,' Evie said, circling the men. 'Which one is Mr Mack? And which one of you is that *awful* criminal?'

'Scoop will know!' Kenny said, and everyone looked at me.

I stared long and hard at both men. They truly were identical!

'Scoop!' one cried. 'It's me, Mr Mack!'

Then the other one turned to me. 'No, Scoop,' he said. '*I'm* Mr Mack!'

'But…' I looked over at Dad. He was just as confused as I was. 'Which one is which?' I asked, looking around, but neither Evie nor Fletcher could tell the difference either.

'Scoop, you have to believe me,' one said, taking a step closer. 'If you don't, *I'll* be sent to prison, but it's *him*, he's the escapee!'

'Scoop, he's lying,' the other one said. '*I'm* Juniper Mack. You know it's me.'

From behind me I heard the trudge of heavy boots making their way up the stairwell. I turned to see Sergeant Andrews. 'Hold it right there,' he shouted. He had seven policemen behind him. But all the constables in the world couldn't help me now.

'Dad!' Evie cried, running over to him.

Sergeant Andrews grabbed his daughter in a tight embrace. 'Oh, thank goodness you're safe, kiddo,' he said, kissing her forehead.

'I'm fine, Dad,' she smiled.

'Sergeant, I know who the culprit is,' I told him.

'It's Harding Mack,' he said, holding up a piece of paper with Harding's mugshot and the word WANTED printed on it. 'We just got informed as we were trying to get to you. One of my constables found this. It was emailed a few days ago, but it must've gone into junk mail. He didn't discover it until just now. If I had gotten it two days ago when I was supposed to, none of this would've happened.'

'Never mind that now,' I said. 'You are correct, the bad guy is Harding Mack. I just… I just don't know which one of these two men *is* Harding Mack!'

'Scoop, look!' one said, taking what looked like an envelope from the other one's pocket. 'It's Fletcher's prize money! He stole it. *He's* Harding Mack, not me!'

'Hey!' the other one said, 'you must've planted that there! When we were rolling around on the floor.' Then he turned to me. 'Come on, Scoop, you must know it's me. I'm Juniper and *he's* Harding.'

'No, *I'm* Juniper and *he's* Harding!'

I swallowed down hard. Sergeant Andrews turned to me. 'Well, Scoop? Which one do we arrest? Which one is Harding Mack?'

I racked my brain for a solution. *Come on, Scoop! You've got this!*

'I've got it,' I whispered to myself, then out loud.

'I've got it!'

'Deivee?' I called to my best friend.

'Rseyr, rssobr?' she replied.

'Dekate dehte denoe dnoe dehte dtfele ddnae dksae dmihe dtahwe dehe dsyawlae ddetnawe dote debe, dtube drevene ddlote denoynae, dkoe?'

'Rerusr rgnihtr, rpoocsr,' she replied.

'What are they talking about?' I heard Sergeant Andrews ask Dad.

'No idea,' Dad shrugged.

Evie walked up to the man on the left and whispered the question in his ear. The man frowned, thought for a moment, and then whispered Evie his answer.

'Dwone dehte denoe dnoe dehte dthgire,' I instructed.

When she had both answers, she skipped over to me.

'Rehtr renor rnor rehtr rtfelr rdiasr rnamerifr,' she told me, 'rdnar rehtr renor rnor rehtr rthgirr rdiasr rnamecilopr.'

At last, I had my culprit!

'Officers, arrest the man on the left,' I instructed. '*He* is your wanted criminal, Harding Mack.'

Back at the police station, Sergeant Andrews said he needed to take official statements from Evie, Fletcher and Mr Mack, which they were all more than happy to provide.

Just as Fletcher had finished giving his statement, Uncle Clive and Aunt Felicity bounded through the door.

'Fletcher!' Aunt Felicity cried. She ran straight across the room and grabbed her son in a hug. Then she kissed him all over his face. Evie and I giggled as Fletcher turned a bright shade of pink.

'Oh, Mum!' he protested.

'Are you okay, son?' Uncle Clive asked, checking Fletcher over.

'I'm fine, Dad,' he smiled.

'Sergeant Andrews filled us in on the phone,' Aunt Felicity said. 'What an ordeal! And this man, this Harding Mack fellow? He'd been living here, these past few days?'

'Yes,' I replied. 'Under the guise of our Mr Mack.'

'There's just one thing I don't understand about all this,' Dad said. 'Why didn't Harding Mack just take the cash and run? Why take Evie and Fletcher with him?'

'It was never about the money, Dad,' I said.

'Harding Mack just needed for us to go searching for them, because he needed to create a scenario where he and Mr Mack could easily be confused for one another.'

'So, when he *did* convince the police, and everyone else, that he was Juniper Mack, the real Mr Mack would go to jail, as Harding,' Evie said. 'And no one would be any the wiser.'

'Correct, my top-notch reporter,' I smiled. 'His main aim was to steal Juniper Mack's identity, and live out the rest of his life here in sunny Higgity Harbour, while *our* Mr Mack rotted away in a prison cell with everyone thinking he was Harding.'

'Precisely,' Sergeant Andrews said. 'And if it wasn't for Scoop, being able to tell the true difference between the two, who knows if his devilish plan might actually have succeeded?'

CHAPTER ELEVEN

TROUBLESOME TWIN MYSTERY SOLVED

ESCAPED PRISONER BACK BEHIND BARS!

By Scoop McLaren

EXCLUSIVE: Just moments ago, at an abandoned beach house on High Cliff Road, far above the peace and tranquillity of Higgity Harbour, Fletcher Stein and Evie Andrews were rescued in what has turned out to be a mystery of gigantean proportions!

Escaped criminal, Harding Mack, was recaptured by police after quietly living in Higgity Harbour under the guise of his twin brother, Juniper Mack, for the past two days. Harding kept his unsuspecting brother at an abandoned beach house.

After Fletcher won the Monster Grommet Title, Harding stole away with Fletcher and *Click!*'s Evie Andrews, who happened upon the crime and tried to intervene. Harding knew the disappearance of the harbour's best young surfer would raise an almighty alarm, taking Evie along, knowing full well the experienced young sleuth would lead investigators to their location.

With a room full of witnesses, and cleverly making certain that he was wearing the exact same clothes as his twin brother, it was up to me, *Click!*'s mystery-solving editor, to tell them apart.

I did so by remembering a little-known fact about Juniper Mack, confided to me just the day before the events. Juniper Mack always wanted to be a policeman! Only the real Juniper Mack knew this answer, thus freeing me to confidently tell the villain from the harbour's trusty surf café owner.

Harding Mack is now back in custody, awaiting transportation to Greenacre Prison, while celebrations for Fletcher's victory today continue. And that, my awesome readers, is what I call another mystery solved! ☺

I wouldn't have blamed Evie, Fletcher *or* Mr Mack if they decided to give Fletcher's party a miss after everything they'd been through, but they all decided it would be a good idea to head to the surf club to celebrate with the waiting crowd.

'So, Harding left the tablet in the boot of the car, knowing full well that it could be used to alert you to our location?' Evie asked.

'Precisely,' I said. 'He knew the police would never stop looking for him, an escapee. By leading us to him, he would be able to make sure the real Mr Mack would end up in prison by confusing everyone and stealing his brother's identity.'

'And Harding would have lived the rest of his days here in Higgity Harbour as Juniper Mack,' Evie added.

'Yes. It was a very elaborate and daring plan; however, unfortunately for Harding Mack, he underestimated one thing,' Kenny said.

'What?' Evie asked.

'Scoop,' he smiled. I grinned.

♥

As we arrived, we met just about everybody at the party – Mrs Lumgarten, Tom Willis, Mrs Bailey,

Jeremiah Turntable and even Imogen Blaxland.

She sauntered over to Evie, Kenny and I as we were grabbing handfuls of potato crisps to eat. *Sleuthing is hungry work!*

'What's wrong, Imogen?' I asked. 'You look like you've lost your last friend?'

'That'd be her *only* friend,' Evie whispered.

'Oh,' she said dramatically, throwing herself down onto a seat next to us, 'it's just positively disastrous, Scoop. As it turns out I'm... I'm *not* related to the royal family. Can you believe it? Not even distantly. Turns out I'm just like you three... plain... ordinary.'

'Jeez, how will you ever manage to go on?' Kenny said, shaking his head and scoffing more crisps down.

'Sorry, Imogen, but it's not so bad, you know, not being related to royalty. Evie, Kenny and I get by okay,' I told her.

'I guess,' she sighed. 'I heard you lot helped solve some... something? Today?'

'Something? *Something?* We only helped the police catch a hardened criminal and solved an actual crime, Imogen,' Evie said. 'All while you were finding out you're just as *ordinary* as we are.'

'Oh, fine, Evie Andrews. Just because your dad's a police—'

'Nobody is ordinary,' I said loudly, trying to calm the conversation. 'We're all special in our own way. Okay?'

'Okay,' Evie said, folding her arms.

'Imogen?'

'If you say so, Scoop,' she said, turning her back on Evie.

Sheesh!

I felt a tap on my shoulder and turned around to see Uncle Clive and Aunt Felicity smiling broadly. They had Fletcher squeezed in between them. After what happened today, they didn't look like they were about to let their only child go anytime soon.

'We owe you everything, sweetheart,' Aunt Felicity said, hugging me.

'And you two as well, Evie, Kenny,' Uncle Clive added. 'We leave here tomorrow knowing that Higgity Harbour is in good hands with you kids around.'

Evie and I smiled at each other. 'Thanks!' I beamed.

'Here she is,' Mr Mack said, walking towards us with my dad in tow. 'Could I have everybody's attention, please?' he called, and the crowd went silent. 'I'd like to propose a toast, to Scoop. If it wasn't for her fine sleuthing skills, for her never giving up, I'd hate to think where Fletcher, Evie and I might be right now.'

'And to Evie,' I added, 'my partner in sleuthing!'

'To Scoop and Evie!' Mr Mack said.

'To Scoop and Evie!' everyone cried.

'Thanks, Scoop,' Fletcher said. 'At first, I thought you were a bit… over the top with your suspicions and funny feelings and everything, but, well… I won't doubt you next time. I promise.'

'Hopefully there won't *be* a next time,' I told him, smiling.

Evie walked over and stood in the middle of the celebration. 'I'd like everyone's attention now, please,' she said. 'I have a special announcement to make.'

'What's going on?' Dad turned to me and asked.

I shrugged. 'Beats me.'

The room went silent and all eyes were on her.

'As you all probably know, Mr Mack and I have never really seen eye to eye,' she started out, 'but this is Higgity Harbour, a place where people always help each other.'

I looked around. People were nodding in agreement. Even Imogen!

'My dad, Sergeant Mick Andrews, and I took the hat around tonight, and, through the generosity of residents and in the spirit of our great founder, Henry

Higgity, we have managed to raise two thousand pounds, which we would like to present to Juniper Mack. We hope it goes some way to keeping the doors of the surf café open.'

'Would you come out here, Juniper?' Sergeant Andrews asked.

I had never seen Mr Mack smile. Not the *real* Mr Mack. Not even in the beach house attic when I proved his innocence. But he was smiling now, and not because of the money. I think he was smiling because of the thought behind it.

He took Sergeant Andrews' hand and shook it, as the room filled with applause.

'*And* we've even prepared a roster,' Evie said, bouncing forward. 'A roster of townspeople who'd be more than happy to help you out at the café, free of charge, just until you get back on your feet, or, if there's ever a time you just want to go fishing,' she smiled.

'Or surfing,' Fletcher added.

'Thank you,' Mr Mack said, his eyes alive with gratitude. Then he turned to the crowd. 'Thank you all!'

'I'm actually a bit sad we're leaving for London, first thing in the morning,' Fletcher said, 'but I think it's fair to say that I will *never* forget this summer in

Higgity Harbour.'

'Back again next year, Fletch?' Dad asked.

'You bet, Uncle Ted,' he smiled. 'Higgity Harbour will always be my second home.'

Evie, Kenny and I stepped out onto the balcony to get some fresh sea air.

'I don't think I've ever seen the moon so full. It looks wicked,' Kenny said as he leaned on the balcony railing.

'It is a perfect night for a celebration,' Evie sighed, twirling around like a ballerina.

'Speaking of the full moon, I guess we can completely discount the theory that everything that went on this week, all the mystery and mayhem, was the work of a silly curse,' I laughed.

Just then, the wind picked up, knocking a large glass mural from the wall. It hit the balcony floor and shattered into a thousand pieces!

Evie squealed and grabbed my arm as the three of us stood, staring up into the night sky…

The next morning after we saw Fletcher, Uncle Clive and Aunt Felicity off, Evie and I hit the waves.

A handful of other surfers were out in the ocean, just like us, taking advantage of a swell that brought in some wicked waves.

I lay on my board and as I felt the ocean rise underneath me, I started to paddle. As the surf caught up to me, I jumped to my feet, up onto my board, slicing along the lip.

Surfing is so cool!

Suddenly Evie came over the top of me and stole my wave – she snaked me! I lost my balance and fell headfirst into the impact zone, the waves crashing on top of me.

I bobbed up from underneath the soup to see Evie, gliding along, unscathed, moving in perfect harmony with the water – dipping, slicing and carving. Then another surfer came and stole her wave, she lost her balance and ended up in the drink herself!

When she emerged, we both jogged in to the beach and threw our boards down onto the sand where my dad and Kenny were waiting for us.

'Did you just see what she did to me, Dad?' I asked as I shook the water out of my ponytail.

Dad just laughed.

'Nice one, Evie,' Kenny grinned.

'What? What did I do?' Evie asked, acting innocent.

'Don't act dumb, you totally just snaked me out there!' I told her as I plonked down onto the sand. Evie looked at me and laughed, and I couldn't help but giggle.

'Well done, girls! That was fun to watch,' Dad said with a smile. 'Kenny and I have to head back to the office though.'

'The news never sleeps!' said Kenny with a wink, as they headed off down the beach.

Ding!

My phone chimed.

'So, what are we going to do this afternoon?' Evie asked, shaking water out of her ears. 'Want to come over to my place? I'm writing a story on…'

It was a message from my mum…

Mum sends me messages every day, sometimes twice a day, but not like this. They are full of 'sweetie' and 'darling', and she always, *always* signs off with, 'I love you'. But not today…

'Scoop?' Evie said as she tapped on my shoulder.

'Oh, huh?'

'What do you think? Will you come over?' Then she frowned.

'Scoop? What's up?' she asked.

'I'm sorry, Evie,' I said, gathering up my board and towel. 'It's… it's my mum… Something's… I… I've got to go…!' Evie was looking worried but nodded.

I checked my watch as I hurriedly made my way home: 10.34 a.m.

Mum sounded awfully strange in her message. I wondered what could be wrong? Whatever it was I'd soon find out – her plane was landing at 12 noon…

ABOUT THE AUTHOR

Helen Castles graduated from Charles Sturt University with a degree in psychology and English Literature.

She divides her time between being a real-life roving reporter for a newspaper and writing about the adventures of detective editor, Scoop McLaren.

She's not fond of technology, is a nervous flyer, loves Foo Fighters music and Bill Murray films, and wants to one day live by the ocean and own a bulldog.

This is her first book series.